'Written with immediacy and poignancy, this is a powerful debut from an exciting and compelling new voice. I loved it.'

SALENA GODDEN

'Tice Cin has arrived. With a style all her own and a confidence that radiates off each page, poetry that renders settings and characters incredibly vivid. No impression will escape you.' DEREK OWUSU

'Thrums with feeling, illustrating the London community with a sharp and confident eye. Her characters are full and sure, and traverse their world with humour, boldness and love. Hope fills these pages.' CALEB AZUMAH NELSON

'A brilliantly enthralling read. Tice Cin's potent crime caper marks the arrival of an intoxicating new voice.'

IRENOSEN OKOJIE

'A beautiful novel – forgiving, meandering and sexy. Tice Cin makes prose ooze and breathe and cook. Her multilingual Tottenham Turkish-Cypriot characters are real people to me now. I love Damla, Cemile and Ayla very much.'

YARA RODRIGUES FOWLER

'Tice Cin is an enthralling voice.' ROGER ROBINSON

'There's always been a poetic, dream-like wonder to Tice's writing. No detail goes unnoticed, unexamined. You see all the tiniest details through her eyes and her words – it's a beautiful gift.' MICHELLE TIWO

'An intoxicating rush of language — and languages. Funny, grimy (in all senses), and driven by a fierce energy, *Keeping the House* holds a deep sadness at its core, but never allows it to overwhelm us, instead finding beauty in balance.'

WILL ASHON

'*Keeping the House* is a thrilling debut by a bold new talent: sparkling, polyphonic and bristling with linguistic energy. Tice Cin has somehow fused experimental writing, crime fiction and the family saga together, while coolly inaugurating the London Turkish novel.' **MATTHEW SPERLING**

KEEPING THE HOUSE

Tice Cin

SHEFFIELD – LONDON – NEW YORK

First published in 2021 by And Other Stories
Sheffield – London – New York
www.andotherstories.org

1 3 5 7 9 8 6 4 2

ISBN: 9781913505080
eBook ISBN: 9781913505097

Editor: Max Porter; Copy-editor: Robina Pelham Burn;
Proofreader: Sarah Terry; Text designed and set in Albertan Pro and
Syntax by Tetragon, London; Cover Design: Olga Kominek, from an
original photograph by Richard Dixon; Printed and bound on acid-
free, age-resistant Munken Premium by CPI Limited, Croydon, UK.

And Other Stories gratefully acknowledge that our work is
supported using public funding by Arts Council England.

For anne. I'm always home because of your voice.
For my family, and our stories.

And for cloudturners.

a cabbage next to a cabbage next to a cabbage
rolls left in the back on a crate with hay
chicken kaka stuck to the bottom third of the leaf

eroin inside

they've been through a lot
looking out at him
this man gingerly
letting a burp escape
out past his shepherd staff
out the truck

he has one more border stop

payment is about three months away
if the plan works – if the money comes

Damla – Daughter of Ayla. Born in 1991.

Ayla – Washes up in high heels. Doesn't like people who think too much.

Zade – OG Tottenham resident. Has a son Erhan's age, named Warren.

İpek – Damla's little sister. Good at hiding before school.

Makbule – Mother of Ayla. Green-fingered. Varicose veins.

Topuz Paşa/Ali – Drives cabbages. Loves bright suits. Has hopes for Ayla.

Sadi – Looks after Nehir supermarket. Always gets pickle juice in his moustache.

Erhan – Son of Ayla, brother of Damla. Has a spiritual connection to Nehir.

Mehmet – Loves coke, relies on Agata too much. Mainlander.

Agata – Crucial side character. Works in Moruk cafe.

Angela – Gives hot Tupperware. Eyes beyond house. Has a little brother, Kwame.

Ufuk – Has two daughters, Filiz and Cemile. Hustles with Mehmet and Ali.

Filiz – Thinks her dad Ufuk sells fruit on Lordship Lane as a job.

Cemile – Cycles too fast. Better behaved than her sister Filiz.

Tulay – Cemile's mum. Strict cleaner. Peacekeeper.

Yusuf – Eighty years old. Key player in Moruk. Shuffles in slippers.

Arjîn – Reports to Babo. Lover of the wrong man's daughter.

Babo/Bekir – Top boss from Mêrdîn. Loves birds.

Panny and his wife Andrea – Greek Cypriot friends of Makbule from Cyprus.

Rohan and Andrej – Love snooker and efficiency.

William – Daydreams on buses. Idolises his mum Sandra.

KEEPING THE HOUSE, 1999

Careful, when you turn your eyes towards someone, you allow them the chance to turn theirs on you. The first time I spoke to my neighbour, I tried to memorise his salt-cracked lips while I had the chance to stare. He called me sweet child, and tucked his thumb under my chin. I asked him why he played his music so loudly. Didn't it hurt his ears? He leant forward, and told me that it feels best when your ears ring sick.

I watched his nails dig into the brick that boxed off his home from mine. His veins jumped and moved in his hands and he gripped the border between us to still himself. Following these veins, from the curves of his triceps to the brick wall, I thought to myself: they are pointed at me.

Whenever I got back home and Anne ^{Mum} wasn't there, my brother and sister would float around me.

Have something cooking by six, she'll be proud.

We would sit with her while she sipped from a glass of rosé. Her hands shook with plans. At the hairdresser's before work, they'd told her she should move out of the area. Business would be better, if her clients were more upmarket – we'd grow up better. When she mentioned it to us, I thumbed my

*Turkish.
All further
translations
are from
Turkish unless
otherwise
stated.*

feet and hoped she wouldn't notice that we'd burnt what was in the oven.

Inevitable. She tucked her hair behind her ears and put down her emptied glass. Asking me to come over to her in the kitchen, she showed me that I hadn't cut the chicken properly: it still had its bum and we don't cook a chicken like that – we are clean people. You can't serve a chicken bum. She sliced greasy, hairy skin from the half-roasted carcass and chucked it in the bin, never dirtying her nails. They were filed down, painted chicken pink, and she refused to let them chip. Her feet were hard from standing all day, still she kept them pretty painted for clients.

The half-cooked chicken bum warmed the bin. Our dinner seemed to taste of its smell. She asked if we had homework to do and we lied so we could stay with her. Grease never touched her lips when she ate. Like her, I tried to eat slowly but the chicken went cold.

She fussed over us on those evenings, washing the dishes and checking we were watching TV in peace. Before bed, when she came to collect us from the sitting room, I asked her what time she'd be coming home tomorrow. She said she's not like those other mums, able to do house stuff all day.

When she came home late, she would walk in smelling of cigarettes. The hard leather of her heels clunked in the hallway before she put her shoes away and put on slippers. As I got older, her late nights gave me time to stay out after school.

THE LITTLE DETAILS OF OUR INTIMACY, 2006

By fifteen I'd make the dishes she taught me. Sweated onions and potatoes. Sulu yemek. Yahni. These were the meals that slid oil into you, that kept you full when you wanted to eat more but couldn't. They heated our skin as the three of us ate on trays, flicking channels until I had to go out. While they waited outside, my friends could see me through the gaps in our curtains. I watched them from the mirror and styled my parting with a rat-tail comb, the skin on my scalp stinging under the pressure. I didn't stop until I had the perfect zigzag. And then I left.

We wore puffer jackets that covered our shapes, and walked in protective clusters until we found benches shrouded by bushes in the estate. Rainwater had gathered on the bench I sat on. It began to soak into my jacket, the nylon holding the cold in. To warm ourselves we took sips of Lambrini until my eyes drooped and everything was peripheral vision and faces meshing together. Sliding off the benches, we were packs of hyenas, ready to make a move. Ambling over to the nearby playground, we sat at the swings with our trainers brushing the ground. I stood on the small paddle seat with my hands wrapped around the rusting chains, watching footwork.

Grime played on a tinny phone. Someone had found a football on the roof of the climbing frame and was kicking it. The ball needed a pump that we didn't have. My friend Angela's dad taught me about *The physics of deflategate*. De-flate-gate. If you put a balloon outside on a cold day, the balloon deflates with the colder temperature. I imagined the softness of the football on their feet, the inflation escaping from pressure and time left out in the elements.The ball in the air – its brief motion of flight – mesmerised me, my face bobbing left to right as a captivated spectator. One of my friends thought to exploit this moment of absorption and pushed the swing from behind. I ended up slung through the air in an arc that matched that of the football. My hands on the tarmac were dotted with mud and ash tipped from the tapping fingers of those too relaxed to move.

The laughter that followed didn't match up with the cracks of blood on my palms. Through embarrassment and dizziness, I managed to make eye contact with my friend Cemile. She grabbed my hand to steady me and suggested I walk home with her. Her hand felt clammy. It didn't occur to me that she was stress sweating. As we walked away from the playground we could hear voices from behind us, telling us we were part-timers. It was the last thing on Cemile's mind.

She told me she was nauseous and needed to book a doctor's appointment or something. Her tongue pushed against her bottom lip as she became increasingly out of breath. We had barely reached the edge of the estate when she asked if she could come and stay at my house. Looking up at Farm looming above us, I felt watched. Even the Peace Mural, with Bob Marley, Gandhi and John Lennon staring benevolently at us, felt like surveillance. So many aunties and olders in these flats, yes. But also, there are the living sounds. Laughter out of context. A man humming somewhere. A door slamming shut. Someone here was upset with Cemile and it felt like they were the source of every sound.

Her house was not far from mine, but my house had no parents inside it. Until midnight, it would just be children. No questions. Just a bed and some rest. She had been avoiding home for a week now, in and out of cousins' houses. They would eventually have to drive her back to her house. Emerging from the car she would see curtains moving, as seated and angered relatives waited inside to see to her. By the end of our short walk home, she'd gone quiet. When we got in she slipped off her shoes and trudged straight upstairs. Out of her puffer jacket and into my pyjamas, she looked her age. In these moments I treasured the little details of our intimacy, even how her big toe had an ingrown nail after being cooped up in too-small trainers. I brought her over to sleep beside me as my little sister İpek peered at her from the ladder of our bunk bed.

When my front door started to thunder I guessed it wasn't for me. Strangled notes came through the letterbox muffler, olive hands pushing through the fringe of hair keeping out the elements. They spoke about how they would break her legs. How Cemile would get the biggest slap around her stupid whore face.

Threats bounced about casually like pins on a map. Exactly how far up they would shove each foot. Her hair? That would be pulled free in chunks of curl. Worst of all, they knew something about her, something that I found out through those choked voices. The street spoke for us before we had to, threatening police and shouting them away – that was the note that we fell asleep on.

ARE YOU BEING
WATCHED ENOUGH?

Mum says what her mum says: the ones who stay pure pave a jewelled path to marriage.

Responsible for guarding ourselves. If I could cuss and cut my eyes at someone, then job done. Some cousins of mine were given a gold belt on their wedding day to show their in-laws how worthy they were. They had successfully rejected their husbands until the wedding night, so they were the good girls. To them, the girls I hung around with were not.

Cemile wasn't watched enough. She'd gotten into the habit of walking up to boys with smoke in her eyes. They called her things that made her feel a heat in her chest and would yank her hand towards them. I used to watch her in confusion, as words and actions refused to match up. She would call them fools and tell them to go away. Still she let them grip the thick flesh of her thighs and hold her tightly against their jackets. The boys would laugh as they took it in turns to squeeze her in bear hugs. The more she squirmed the more they would tell her how cute she was. They loved her for her smiles and playful rejections and they loved her more for the way she kept going back. What would be humiliating to some was a game to her. Her sense of humour rang raw as she told jokes that kept them laughing, with her, not at her. They would take their hats off to perch them on her hair, saying they suited her better. I grew respect, witnessing the way she operated. To her, hands on thighs meant nothing more than play and fun. She knew when to stop. She'd return to me. Always with something new. The smell of vodka at her lips. Something drawn on her hand. A hoodie that she'd never return.

Cemile's graveyard detour:
All the people buried there, no family left to visit any more.
No place else to go, meet a boy here.
She told me he gave soft kisses.
I was a good friend so I stood guard.
Dirt never touched her trainers –
immaculate, five white stripes.
Soft kisses.
Gentle tread.
What if, Cemile?
Lies have a way of bursting in your mouth.
Her mouth, holding secrets, not the same as lying.
No, not the same.

I asked her when she started. Back to being twelve. Weekends, she would go to her auntie's home to see her family in Broadwater Farm. They had a flat that had two large rooms, a small kitchen and an even smaller bathroom. The lift for Northolt had been left busted for longer than she could remember.

Cue Cemile: up a staircase that smells of bleach and cheese. Can of Charlie Red with her at all times, spraying to the eighteenth floor.

A new pair of shoes on the landing one night, one 10s with mud slicked over the bottom.

Kitchen first, prepare sweets for the visitors.
Bring them out.
Follow a rumble.
Voices going with the football on the screen.

Only one of the voices thanked her; she tried not to stare at its owner but couldn't avoid blushing as she noticed drying mud on the young man's trousers. When she returned to the kitchen she was given a baby cousin to hold. He tugged at her hair until a little tuft of it was yanked free. All she could think was that she would now look terrible. Her hair had sprung loose from its bun. She would walk past the room with the child hushing and humming her to sleep but, really, she was there to catch the back of his head, or the way he leant forward to see the screen closer.

At night, the two rooms were transformed. Airing cupboard emptied of starched sheets and beds made on the floor. Cemile lying shoulder to shoulder with her aunties, feeling the feet of little children draped over her legs. No sleep. Cupboards lined the back of the room and lace nets hung from them, swaying slowly in the breeze of the night. One had been left open and the scent of mothballs cut through the oil in the air. She saw a shadow on the cupboard before firm hands under her armpits. He pulled her through the sleeping bodies and past the men's room, the room she'd been told to stay out of. In the kitchen, she saw his face properly for the first time, lit up by his Nokia.

He blinked too often, smiled too little.
Be quiet.
Sink
teeth into his shoulder, so real it's sigh hushing
Smell
his sweat with her auntie's cooking
Hot air of visiting bodies.
Moment gone too soon.

As she lay back down on the blanketed floor with her family she learnt that she was made for secrets. Something told her it would never happen again with him. He wouldn't return. She wasn't sure why she felt relief – when she tried to recount the act it was like her memory was failing her, there just wasn't enough sweetness to remember.

When she woke the next day, her grandmother called her over and slapped her. She looked down at herself. Every Turkish girl gets slapped on the first day of her period. She was told that her cheeks would always stay red this way. A twelve-year-old given towels that stuffed her underwear tight and she changed them proudly. She hid bloodless pads in the bin for a week and prayed that her mum wouldn't check it.

That was before she gelled down her curls, with thick eyeliner swept in manic lines towards the sky. Her chest now had a soft glimmer of hair and a mole just before the bra line. She leant forwards when she spoke so that her breasts spilled ahead, as though rushing to greet you. I did what I could do to impress her. It was as though she was always above me.

Her smell spoke another language. She lent me a cardigan once and I wore it home, cocooned in her. When I got home my mum saw me, took it off me, washed it and hung it over the balcony, clean cotton smell drowning her out. As I ironed it before its return, my fingers rested over the worn buttons and a rip in the armpit that was barely discernible. Before I gave it back I sewed it up and she noticed, a half-smile on her face before she rammed it into her small rucksack and hugged me.

SMALL ROUTINES, 2006

A cockroach infestation started in the house and I didn't know how to solve it, so we became accustomed to them. The way they snuck into my house, in the room I shared with my little sister, helped me.

Me, small.
Me, in the cracks in the wall.
Cockroach in the cracks with my lovers.
Emerging at night to steal food.
Rolling in secret places.

Dancing in my room gave me a warmth in the stomach, a pride that I could do more than just wine. I made my body a wave, treading softly inside the songs, so that the only one aware of me was İpek. With these tracks, I could move (without restraint) the same parts that my mother had taught me to swirl in belly dance. Control in the core, between letting go and holding tight. My partner was a shadow filled with whoever I'd smiled at during the day. I pictured men moving towards me, like in the videos I waited for on night TV. İpek kept asking to join in. I'd carry her down from the bunk and spin her till her feet were rubbed red from the rough carpet.

İpek asked me why I was so happy today, too young to know the thing in my chest that made me want to pull off my skin and bounce along the streets. I wanted to be seen.

But my feet threw shadows under my bedroom door when I moved. I hated it.

.

On the walk home from school I picked up my little brother Erhan from primary.

Two bottles of blue Panda pop to drink before we got home. Our tongues, slick sugary algae.

I loved how intently he listened as I spoke, as I told him.

Why he should always look at the ground as he was walking so he didn't catch the wrong eye. The perk of this, I assured him, was that you never stepped on loose gum and puddles. Sometimes you would even find money.

I respected it when he ignored my advice and only in those moments did I feel that he could be grown. By Year 6, his eyes would tip up from the street, with a calm face finding the producers of any smells he'd caught while looking down. You can't teach that stuff. In these moments we would stay calm and walk slowly, feeling home ahead of us in the pits of our tummies.

I took him to get barbecue thighs from Dixy Chicken. Slipped him chips as we got closer to the house. That day my neighbour was waiting on his brick wall. He told us that my mum wasn't home, leant over and took a can of Lilt from the plastic bag in my hand. I savoured a half-chewed chip in my mouth, thanking fortune that he had not touched our food.

25

We went to open the front door and I felt a tap at my elbow before I slammed it shut. My hands were starting to grease from the smeared plastic handles of a takeaway and stress.

İpek was home sick that day, starving by the time we got in. I upturned the food onto the kitchen table and we ate from the cardboard, rubbing it red with sauce and chips.

All we had to do was stay in one piece and eat together.

In moments like this I would look at the kitchen window and imagine I had a neighbour who loved me nice. He would watch me as I neatly picked demerara skin from the chicken. I played a game with myself, avoiding sucking the barbecue from my nails in case a mysterious lover was testing me from a distance. When I came out from that fantasy, I would begin eating again with a renewed energy, letting my cheeks stain like my siblings did. Happy to be alone and to wash my hands only when the meal was done. All we had to do was stay in one piece and eat together.

That night I go to my friend Angela's. Her name is Araba too, for Tuesday, but a lot of us change our names around here. Though her younger brother Kwame never did. She lives in one of the ground-floor flats on the farm. We listen to Déjà Vu (Nine Two Three!), Venom Krew crackling into existence, slither planting their hold on me. Her mum makes us peanut soup, the base taken from the freezer and heated for my last-minute visit. We sit around the table after we eat, until it's 'dad is coming home soon'. He drives trains for a living and needs his privacy when he comes home. It is stressful work, they miss him and he needs them. I leave and walk home that night with the smell of oil in my hair, pulling my plait from the inside of my coat. I hold it to my nose like a mask and take quick strides in the cold. Home is two roads away and there are whispers at my back. It is late. I should be home. Before walking into the house I look up to the top floor to see shapes at the window and a man seated in front of the corner shop, watching along with me, his face in an unapologetic leer.

Times like this I wish I had another face.
Turn: cheeks weeping maggots, eyes hollowed out.
Serves you for looking.

Instead, I hide my face. Fear speaks too quickly – better to slow its path, eyes averted.

In the house, I smelt a visitor. Kitchen. A man pinching a spliff between his fingers, corner of my eye. He was rocking himself against the weakened fence in my garden while staring in. I checked the back door was locked and brushed my fingers over the chipped paint of the windowsill, willing him to walk away. As if he could hear my thoughts, my neighbour flicked his ash on the grass and loped back over to his house.

It felt pointless to speak or do. You turn off the lights and get used to finding your way back to bed. I played R&B that night, songs prepping me on a low volume until the CD timed out. No repeat. I fell asleep before the last song, catching İpek's face hanging down from the top bunk, staring at my feet. The only thing she could see, poking out from the covers that hid my face. I wiggled my toes to seem happy until the music stopped my thoughts.

BREAD KNIVES AND
LITTLE HEELS, 2007

A Peugeot 106 laid a trail for another car to follow. It set off loudly down Tottenham High Road, four men inside, rattling past the police station before people lost sight of it.

Earlier in the night, these four men had waved one ticket at a bouncer, demanding four-for-one entry. They promised that with them inside, the whole place would light up. One of the men spoke in the riddles of a sativa high. With each of the bouncer's rejections, his concentration broke and came back in. Gradually, his fingers carved through the air like carrion picking bones, sharp and deliberate. He stood in a halo of smoke, watched by girls in little heels and jeans, holding cigarettes in their hands, mouths ajar.

Inside, the dance floor was carpeted and it smelt of peppermint. It was ravey, with an hour in the middle for a cypher, focus turning. When the beats shift into another wave, you have to catch the moment where your moving changes, correct yourself.

Dancing as exercise:
carry on till you're gasping

water water
elbow-tappers popping up
cups of water, second-hand flavour
bit of a twist

I learnt not to breathe as I sipped at strange glasses, otherwise I would begin to picture the gaping, moustached mouth that might have hovered over the same glass earlier. The tongue that may have rested on the rim of the cup. Or the fingers that touched the sides, warm from the iced urinals.

Outside, the boys were still trying to get in. One was offended by his treatment. With each look hot, then cold, he kept his feet fidgeting while he reached into his pocket and took out a bread knife. The serrated edges slid back and forth into the bouncer's stomach, tugging at sinew and detaching flesh from bone. As though peeling away, his body folded into an 'S' shape, head onto the pavement. The man slipped his weapon away and sprinted back to his car.

Ducking out through the same fire exit we'd used to sneak into the building, we managed to avoid the rush. I saw one of my friends disappear in the panic, throwing out his fists to keep himself standing. He reappeared later to meet us, in McDonald's waiting for warmth. Adrenaline sat in my mouth, I drank strawberry milkshake and let it rest coldly each time before swallowing.

It was Cemile's last week in London and she wouldn't stop eating. I kept telling her that there was a McDonald's in North Cyprus but she told me that the meat tasted different there and pulled apart chicken nuggets to show me. I counted the number of homeless people buying a burger from the saver menu and finishing them before they'd reached the exit.

On the walk home, someone ahead threw trainers into a tree and ran into a house.

They hung there until the neoprene sheen faded. These trainers marked the distance I had left to travel home, the last quarter of my walk, and of course I always thought of that night when I saw them hanging there.

The night the bouncer was attacked:

Club at sixteen.
Cemile's bitten nails.
Chicken into thumb-sized pieces.
Cemile eating with her eyes closed.
Cheeks fatter than before.
Little groups shivering tables
folding money
recounting
fragmented cycles, making sense.
It was this, it was this too, and it was this.
Eavesdrop so much you think you saw it.
Dancing during knives.
Eavesdrop so good you tell it better yourself.
Eyes closed in McDonald's.
Tired chicken face.
Retell it so it's yours and it's yours now
and it's yours now.

IT SHOULD LINGER
ON THE TONGUE, 2007

When Cemile left she did not contact me. I bought a Lycamobile SIM card to call her with but each call was answered by relatives of hers explaining that she was busy, or tired, or out. Money wasn't there for me to follow her. The emptiness was made better by Angela. She would bring her little brother to my house and food from her mum. Bean and plantain, or big meat stews. The returned Tupperware was stained red despite our attempts to clean them. It reminded me of home. Our Tupperware is just the same.

Angela could talk. Her stories made me think of planes and a wage. The type of luxe-living that led you by the hand into music video territory. Her dad put his wages straight into her head. He had been buying her *National Geographic* magazine since she was twelve. She told me mad things. She planted pictures of enemies in my mind, enemies I didn't know I needed to have. These soya bean producers were worse than my neighbour. It was nice to hear her plans though. She compared her future self to a Morpho butterfly, a bit alien and impossible to ignore – flying down on them with Tottenham logic, protecting the trees.

She sounded as though she was always agreeing with herself. Her hands tapping my knee for approval at 120 beats per minute told otherwise. The only way she would stop with the tapping was if I made a point of telling her how good her ideas were.

When the stories returned to our reality, they would change shade. We would talk about the vast expanses of Hackney Marshes – how corpses secretly buried there had made certain sections of it into landmarks, things to point at in hushed tones. It was littered with bodies as much as a plague pit. Apparently. Or we would fill in the gaps of local narrative around all the boarded-up houses. The council boards them up to keep out the undesirables but some of the houses seem to glow at night. We would concoct tales of green women stirring heads in cauldrons or men torturing each other because of a bad drug deal, like Babo. We've heard all about the hooks and buzzers them men use.

.

Anne leaves the house first thing in the morning. If I woke from the sound of the door slamming I would feel some kind of gut punch, a sense of loss maybe, and jump from bed to see her walking away, though often I didn't even catch her turning the corner. I might hover in the hallway wondering what to eat before going back to bed. We woke late to skip meals. When we got up there'd be pound coins scattered on the sitting room table, and I would put that towards bits. Or go down the sofa for extra coins. Always milk for cereal, it would keep us until the evening.

A daytime run to the market. You have to be one of the first ones in. There are less gossips in the morning. The shop is invariably packed with Haringey's Cypriot community and they all ask me how my mother is doing. It must be hard raising all those kids alone. The fruit stalls had gathered us all together: we picked at taro and long red peppers, elbow to elbow with each other.

These interactions, space shared with the people hustling up against me, were comforting. We moved in parallel lines, coasting the shoreline of baskets for good finds. It made me feel like I was part of something computational– we were being cued up into ascending actions. I would imagine the contents of everyone's fridges. I noticed a few people picking up things without testing them, watermelons going unknocked, mint that was not rubbed. I felt dirt on my fingers from delving into a pile of lemons and picked up six for a pound.

When Anne brought me to these markets she'd show me how to taste spices for quality. She would crouch near burlap sacks full of Urfa biber, shaking a small amount of the maroon spice from the scoop to her hand. Wetting her finger, she explained that when you tasted it, it should linger on the tongue, raisin sweet – and you should be able to taste the respectable lineage that the pepper had come from.

In final year, I'd think about home as soon as I had lunch, settling down with a tray of food. In a reverie induced by a particularly grey burger, I met William. He wore clean shoes and aftershave. Offered me some packed lunch, I wanted a recipe for everything until he became a third party, between his mum and me. He'd inspired something in me that made my cooking turn sweeter when I got home. I baked desserts for İpek and Erhan until they started to feel mild dread watching me crush pistachios with a rolling pin and lovingly scatter them over syrupy semolina.

I pictured sugar spores picking themselves up from the thick cane sugar and spinning like dandelion seeds out of my kitchen window, towards his bedroom window. Sugar landing on his forehead. Wiping it off like sweat he would taste my adoration. Cooking a waiting game; imaginary plans cut and kept in flour.

Soon he asked to meet me after school and so one day a week I'd be late home, getting back just minutes before Mum.

William and I got to know each other cloud-watching in the park. When he said my name he often smiled afterwards. I wanted to get more familiar with him, count the holes in his socks and go through his DVDs. He started to take me home and feed me, his eyes darting curiously around my face as I ate stacks of cassava bread and fried okra with shrimp. I had more than I wanted, rude to eat too much, rude not to eat.

His mum was shy to speak and so her son spoke for her, always-kind words followed by a gentle pat of the shoulder before she disappeared into the living room. She would play the TV loud. The soundtrack to my evenings with William would be the sound of movie-women or police sirens wailing. On my way out I would creep past her sleeping body to turn the TV off. I never got why she gave the bedroom to her son or why he took it. She slept on a pull-out that felt too flimsy for her body and kept a two-litre bottle of cream soda by her pillow. No one else could sleep as good.

William's mother:
proof you can have more than one family
in her little kitchen to fry sprats
so easy to make, just wash them in lime,
salt, pepper
in the plate, raw onion.
Metemgee, add duff to the pot.
Swallow some bones, pick some.
Oil wet your fingers from picking.

Like my family, ingredients relocated from dish to dish.
Sprats fried one day and turned into a smoky fish stew the
next. William had a fear of his mother that meant he could
only plead with his eyes for me to come next door. I would
pretend I didn't notice him, standing unbidden by the door.
His room had none of the joy I found in the kitchen, it was so
quiet, except for his breathing and the TV through the walls.

POT BELLY, SUMMER OF 2008 (THINKING BACK, WAY BACK TO '74)

Somewhere in time, I found myself gaining weight. On my stomach at first but then I kept putting it on, until I couldn't see my hipbones any more. Sat with my feet propped against the radiator I would read recipes given to me by friends and their families.

Angela mumzy
30-Jul-2008 17:34
Miss, you can't forget the shito.. basic..
OPTIONS   REPLY   BACK

I was found like that one morning by my mum. She walked into the kitchen and stared at a pair of thighs leaking into the wicker dining chairs. Leaning over, she poked them with her long nails, sniffed and sat with me.

My mother used to have a pot belly, she told me (time for her life story):

She ate to adjust to change. Her dad died and left behind a house in Tottenham. It was the only property their family had left after the war in Cyprus. Following '74, barely any paperwork was recognised as proof of ownership for the land they had bought on the island. Newly widowed, her mother, Makbule, would queue with hundreds of people in line at the belediye başkanlığı *Council office. Site for conducting the* in Nicosia. She eventually claimed *affairs of the municipal boundaries* a one-bed on the north side of the island. The buildings in the new village had none of the red-brown of the straw and mud bricks of her childhood, and she missed her cabbage plants. After ten years of waiting for administrative powers to arrange themselves, Cyprus no longer felt like home. Turkish Cypriots had been coming from the forties to London, another home. Some distant family soon invited Nene *Grandma* and Anne to join them in London on visitors' visas. Behind them, the small bungalow was left to her grandmother's niece to watch in their stead.

Just as Ayla left Kıbrıs, new universities opened across the island. Doğu Akdeniz. Girne Amerikan ... Her teachers had told her she was smart enough to go to any of those. She had stayed on at Türk Maarif Koleji one extra year to pass her English writing exams and told herself that she was made for something bigger. Someone had once said she even had the looks to be an anchorwoman on Bayrak Televizyon.

After her final exams she was left in the Green Line city, waiting for a cousin from the village to come and collect her from the school's boarding house. Arm in arm, she and her friend Emine (also waiting for a lift) would walk, holding books of radical poetry. This poetry had been passed from bed to bed around the boarding room; starting with the older girls until eventually reaching Ayla. Neşe Yaşın was her favourite – a woman angry, right there on the page.

Sometimes poetry wasn't enough. Poetry could be too coy about fantasies. When this happened, Emine would take her hand and pull her towards the local newsagent's to buy a foto roman – a pamphlet of serial dramas, filled with couples clinging to one another in passion. They would trace the pages, call themselves Claudia or Maria, and escape. Foto roman was unreal real, away from the procession of tanks that inhabited the daily rhythm of school life.

One Lady and One
Moment of Chance

BIR KADIN VE BIR TESADÜF

Valeria	Marina Coffa
Fabio	Franco Gasparri
Monica	Isabella Savana
Gabriele	Gianfranco de Angelis
Olga	Mirella Mereu
Luigi	Claudio de Renzi
Antonio	Nando Sarla

FABIO: Nereye sinemaya mı?

VALERIA: Bu gece hastaba-kiciliga basliyorum. Akil hastanesinde. Kücük bir sürpriz . . .

FABIO: Where are you going? Cinema?

VALERIA: Tonight I'm starting my care for the poorly, the mentally unwell. I have a little surprise . . .

•

In the middle of a row of clothes stores, you would find the helvacı. Everything built from cool stone, at the grinders, the helva makers would stand mixing. From a churning wheel the smell of tahın carried in the air: sugar, vanilla, chocolate. The brown aprons worn by the helvacılar would flutter behind them as they cut out blocks of helva into kilos. She used to want to marry those men, too. It was the way they told her 'afiyetler olsun', wishing her good health as they passed her the package. They spent time on the words. She would sit and share a whole block with Emine, singing their traditional helva-eating anthem, 'Helvacı' by Mavi Işıklar:

Helvacı helva	Helva place, helva
Şeker lokumlu helva	Helva with sugary lokum
Kendir tohumlu helva	Helva with hemp seeds

They wanted a high. Wanting hemp helva and singing about it wasn't yet in the category of things you shouldn't say. If the Turkish Beatles can say it then it's probably OK. The words became a mantra: as ceremoniously as Ayla touched her hand to her ear every time she passed a cemetery, so too would she sing this song with Emine. It took them four minutes to reach a bench they liked (also two choruses of 'Helvacı').

BANDABULLIYA

Olives, cracked, green
Lefkara lace

Mosque
Mosque goers,
Viewing spot
taps

Coffee stall

Bus station /
Han

Snacks on wheels:
Bomba donut
Pide, köfte.

Not many people went to that mosque for dusk prayers. There
was another one — only a five-minute walk away — that more
people visited. This place had a holier feel to Ayla. From her
dorm room, she would hear it call to her every night. In those
moments she made a choice to fall back asleep but not before
thinking about another kind of life. A life where she joined
in at prayer time.

·

When Ayla first moved to the UK in 1986, Broadwater Farm was brushed with the glow of attention. Her home with Makbule overlooked the estate. Farm seemed like the only place that was buzzing when she moved to Tottenham. One second she'd see a man singing and smiling, holding a can of Tennent's and a stickered-up boom box, a whistle round his neck. If you turned in another direction, the elevated walkways would open out to old couples bitterly walking their dogs. There was an Alsatian who would vault benches to run to Ayla.

Her house, on the other hand, felt . . . run down, by years of neglect, and being taken up by squatters who didn't leave until Haringey Council finally forced their hand. Ayla ended up doing the type of deep clean that leaves you with a mild cough from bleach fumes. This is the pot belly time. She would finish her day, sit hunched over a pot of stew chicken and shred the skin into mounds, heap in her hands and eat.

The first time she went food shopping with her mum, Ayla met a woman about her age who wore clothes Ayla would have worn if she could have. She liked to be called Zade. One of the first things Zade said to my mum was that the road she lived on was where an old lady's head had been found speared by a curtain rod. My mother made a friend. She liked honest people. They bonded over both being relatively new to London, and music that reminded them of other times, Esmeray and Stamma Haughton. Two island babies that kept waking up to a view of English concrete. It was Zade who decided our house should be painted magnolia to liven it up a little. Zade, too, who helped her get a couch with bunches of grapes and liana printed over it.

The difference between Ayla's public life and home life was stark. She spent her spare time introducing herself to locals, from the women who ran the nearby off-licence to the Turkish Cypriot family with a cafe a couple of roads away. Her group of friends grew thin and slow. After visiting she'd return home to my nene, slowly readjust to a lifestyle of yellowing skin and varicose veins. Makbule wore the face of a widow in a time warp, reliving the moment of her husband's death repeatedly until she couldn't serve coffee to guests without it bubbling over and smelling of coal. Still, guests came.

A couple called Panny and Andrea, who knew her before the war, before England, would sit and speak Greek Cypriot with Nene until she laughed. Zade did the same. But there were days when company was too much and Makbule would shut herself in her room, pull its heavy lace nets shut and lie in bed until the room smelt of urine and rang with her muffled voice, its strangled notes caught in a pillow. My mother become stronger the more she had to help. Makbule would lie in the garden on a picnic blanket, her swollen legs propped on a pillow while her daughter planted grapevines and pruned old cherry trees.

Makbule's legs bore the strain of crouching in waterlogged land, standing for long hours milking cows and ploughing melon fields. The doctors also spoke about her kidneys, equally worn. She called my mother her miracle child, something given in old age to show her life could still be precious when everything else is taken away.

SWEET ENOUGH
TO ESCALATE

The empty rooms of a big house can make you ache to fill them. My mother started to ache daily. First the feeling started in her feet, then her heart would beat so much her chest felt crushed. Realisation: she was finally in the position to live out the lives of the women she'd admired in foto romans.

Being the heroine of your own love story starts with a belief in magnetism, pulling the right corresponding elements towards you and somehow sifting out the debris.

She'd been given a job in a post office on Mount Pleasant Road, handing out giros to customers who would then spend their cheques in the shop. They'd buy Uncle Ben's rice and clothes for their children, with tiny Velcro-strapped shoes – the sturdiest option – worn long past one year too-small.

In 1988, Zade asked her to her first house party by Farm, and life seemed to turn from black and white to Technicolor. Anyone rejected from the Tottenham Ritzy was welcome there, DJs set up playing dancehall and dubs. She met my father propped up half-asleep against a red-stained bathroom mirror. His body was hot from sweat and he smelt like Old Holborn. She needed the toilet so much that she had to roll him out of the room and slam-lock the door. Face washing, she left the tap to run over the shards of broken glass and wet stubs inside it. The water kept running, feeling warm on her fingers, running over them until it split into tributaries off of her hands. The hissy tap was a synthesiser intro, building towards something, and only interrupted by the drumming of my dad at the door.

When she opened the door, he noticed the glass in the sink had cut her hand. He placed his hand on it to stop the flow. It was a small cut, but the salt grime of his hands stung her into fascination. She let him hold her hand, and walked with him into a garden full of sleeping faces and dancing bodies. He danced. To her it was like watching a man belly dance, the way he shimmied towards her with those serious eyes. Her laughter surprised him. He asked why he had never seen her before. Her accent and the colour of her navel (darker than her face, it seemed to have locked in an entire childhood of sunlight) told him the answer. His hand reached for her stomach like she was his pregnant wife. He cupped it with one hand while the other pulled her towards him for a kiss. The taste tanged in her mouth and she couldn't place it. All she knew was that she didn't like the way he tasted, as much as she knew that she wanted to feed him. She wanted him to taste like her cooking instead.

Ayla had decided to be a practical woman. She went to work the next morning then returned home, rubbed Makbule's legs with Hirudoid cream and then cooked dinner. Her patience felt like white noise. She didn't need to wait any more. After a few weeks she got a knock at her door, a man with bad breath and good hands who asked her to take a walk. The neighbours had yet to hang their heads out of their windows and she left the house while her mother slept in her room.

They walked to a Wimpy burger bar on Tottenham High Road and he ordered her a banana milkshake. She sipped on it as if it was the yoghurt drink ayran, disappointed by its sweetness. While she drank, he ate chips. She watched the gold rings on his fingers shake whenever he picked up a chip. He was wearing tight beige slacks and a fitted shirt with a dense bougainvillea print. You could tell it was a good shirt from the way it was cut, its cufflinks embroidered with a 'V' and two stripes. He told her he liked Naf Naf, Versace and Levi. He lived in a bedsit with a literature student from UCL who forced books on him like a mother trying to fatten up her child. He taught her about technologies of the self – how to become embodied in the act of dressing smart. He managed his body by exercising twice a day. When he woke up he did four sets of ten pull-ups, and then he exercised his lower lats with typewriter pull-ups, moving side to side until his arms felt tired and sore. Hair was important too – he combed oil through before blow-drying it into shape.

Outside the Wimpy, a stream of Spurs fans spilled into the pub across the road, and his attention went to the window for a moment. Antennas out. He stayed quiet, until the pavements outside were almost empty. My mother was intrigued by the way football fans all blended into each other as though their faces could have been made of papier mâché. I think that made my father feel special, that he wasn't one of those men in her eyes.

To him, the immediate bodily pleasures of good clubs, and the right kind of women, was an answer. He did not make plans. He tossed his wishing coin into the mouths of strangers, absorbing their jokes and touches, walking away feeling pumped. That evening the roles seemed reversed. He was this open vestibule of knowledge, a sophisticated chip and milkshake buyer who really knew London. But he didn't know what she knew about life. When they met she would ping strawberries at him and complain about the smell of oil in his hair. They would kiss to the sound of her giggling. The ridiculousness of two faces smashing together in front of the whole world. She took him to the markets with her and made him hold paper bags stuffed to the brim with vegetables, poking him in the moustache. Can't take yourself too seriously. Even when he began to lose concentration she would give him pilavuna bread or pastry stuffed with nor ricotta-style cheese. His lips tasted more like her the longer they spent together, and eventually their kisses were sweet enough to escalate.

The first time she went to his home the mess pleased her: a helpless man is a grateful man. She slid into the Archway flat with a degree of comfort, draping her clutch bag over the bedpost. Next door, a line of books belonging to his roommate Eric separated two couches. Paisley patterns swam across the surface of their dimpled brown wallpaper. The kitchenette was clean except for a few tea-stained spoons in the sink, and she found the homeliness in it, even in the bathroom.

His room smelt good like him, its duvet thin but floral. She wrapped herself in it and covered her hair in the style of her great-grandmother. His laughter felt genuine. Under the bed, he kept paintings collected from the houses of friends who had paid for things with possessions. Dust on her back, she looked over them ... How many were naked women, how many were fractured landscapes in cubes and blocks, how many were memories? With everything in the home now introduced to her and all comments made, there wasn't much else left to do but look at one another. At twenty-one her face had grown long, with no more fat hanging off the cheekbones – that had migrated to her thighs, which were almost bursting out of white trousers. Flesh you could clutch and slide your thumbs off. He kissed her in ways she had only known the look of, sinking ways. She didn't see him again for months.

He always returned. His reappearances, his cajolement and inescapable wheedling, were accompanied by Ayla's voice rising up and up, eventually settling on a modicum of compliance. He had police following him around, he didn't have a passport and had lived in a shed for a month. Another time, he said he had to drive to France to collect six months' worth of sun-dried tomatoes, hiding his haul on the way back so nobody would try to rob him. The excuse that left his mouth the most was that he had been unwell, had gone to his mother to get better and that one day maybe the two women could meet each other.

The gaps were sometimes worth the wait. Though he returned to her skinnier and hungrier each time, in show-man's clothes. He had the maniacal energy of a man who had been kept in jail for too long without company, spending too much money on his girl or kissing her mid-meal with a mouth full of jerk beef patty.

Subtlety was not something she was completely familiar with anyway. She lived for six months without a TV when she first came to London; they were too busy making a home. But this changed the day a satellite was installed by her cousins. Cousins so distant that they charged her a third extra on the standard price, to make their house a Pat Butcher-style earring on the end of their street. And so a specific kind of therapy was discovered. Makbule was a bloodthirsty TV watcher. She found equal comfort in watching Cüneyt Arkın karate-chopping evil wizards in half and telenovela romances where young girls lost their virginity before marriage and ended up murdered or working in brothels. Babysat by the TV, Makbule would mutter disbelief that such a beautiful woman as Hülya Avşar would willingly play a victim of rape – she could be acting in comedies.

Ayla left this routine to go out.

It was the later part of their dates that became her favourite. They would start simple, Burger King on wooden benches overlooking the skyline, before a night out. He instructed her to dress special, taking her to the Mud Club in Leicester Square to see Mark Moore spinning soul and funk. Other women there were casual, shredded 501s and white pointy heels, but those women didn't suit him the same way. He'd walk in wearing a fifties work suit, soon shed to its constituent parts: an open shirt and slacks. The music policy ran from hip-hop to high camp. The sort of sounds that could clear a hangover immediately, Public Enemy's 'You're Gonna Get Yours' switching to Farley 'Jackmaster' Funk. She started to build a sense of the scene; soon she didn't need her escort.

At night her mum would call for her without response.

Her boyfriend was a sleepy-eyed man. He took her out but inside he was waiting for some silence. When they got back in, he would clamber on top of her, to admire her in the context of his bed frame. They continued to see each other intermittently in this same way for a couple of years, until her legs swelled and her stomach peeped out from T-shirts.

My mother did not expect much to change when he saw her big like this. After they had been apart for months, he called on her and took her to his flat. She was holding a big bag of pastries to put in his fridge but it was unplugged, warm and orange inside. He was withdrawn, skinny-cheeked. He still looked like her lover. His lips weren't cracked and his skin wasn't sallow. She asked him to look at her and he rubbed her belly gently, but there was pain in his face. He was missing something. So desperate for that something that he whipped off his shirt, sat on his bed and wrapped his belt around his elbow. She was used to needles, you get to see plenty when your mother is in hospital as much as Makbule was. What she was not prepared for was seeing his face change. She had adjusted to the thought of other women becoming a possible wedge between them but her imagination hadn't taken her to this.

The luxury of leaving the room. Vomit.

When she returned to his room he was already asleep, breathing so slowly as to seem non-existent. She tried to wake him. His breaths seemed to speed when she held his hands and so she did, leaving when she felt he looked alive. She couldn't pretend it hadn't happened, but didn't know how to help. Enough things made sense now to see that he wouldn't find the help he needed from people she knew. Before she walked out she left a plate of börek by his side, with a note telling him that he was always welcome in her home.

My father a faint memory . . . someone in my siblings' faces . . .
to my mother, an ectoplasm . . . long as he turned up again,
    it would all be all right . . . everything's gonna . . .
        Scooby-Doo ghost man I never managed
            to chuck any flour on . . .
whole childhoods part-time, still she would not let us say it . . .
    to say it is to diminish him – always big man in her
    eyes . . . proved it on a few occasions . . . not around
    enough to make it mean enough . . . lived in absence . . .
ashtrays on the window ledge . . . washed summer clothes,
            in the cupboard all season.

When I was born, a great many guests stopped their visits to our household. They looked, and asked questions, but didn't come in for tea. On Ayla's days off she opened her windows and left the kettle on the stove all day, leaves steeping. She imagined whispers going past her front door. What do you expect when you leave a village girl in London with just her mum? Soon she stopped brewing tea. If a guest did come, she would simply wash the dust off a teabag and pop it in a cup.

Makbule was not ashamed of her daughter's pregnancy. If anyone tried to give her bother when my siblings were born, she would just tell Ayla not to pay it any mind. To cook instead.

Through Ayla's pregnancies she kept up her shifts at the post office. Nene watched us, sick. The first thing I remember about her are legs threaded with spider veins. Her smell: heparinoids and cooking oil. She would stay in the kitchen whenever my mother returned home, sat in the armchair by the fridge, offering a running commentary on the cooking. The two women cooked together. My mother measured spices as her mother advised, with the lines on her palm. Everything made in that kitchen was personal to her. When she cooked for her family, she cooked memories. Makbule always mopped up what had stuck to the pan with bread. Butter and Urfa chilli, bandırma, she called it. Her husband had loved these recipes.

At seventy-six, she began to hallucinate, often after a particular sound or smell. A bowl of fasulye would transform from beans into mud that she would sift through, looking for someone. The sound of the ceramic, scraped by cutlery, played on Ayla's ears until she took the bowl away. When she became listless and wouldn't eat, she was spoon-fed.

—It's like you're force-feeding me my past.
—Lutfen, Anne. Just try.

Makbule hit the spoon out of her hand, and went to her bedroom, shutting the door behind her.

DAMLA: SEMOLINA HELVA AND OTHER FUNERAL TREATS, 2001

At the funeral people are scattered around in small groups, their heads following the loudest streams of conversations or the loudest cries. They are either guided by grief or they are grief's voyeurs.

The wind blew the pollen from some orchids into my mother's face and I wipe the ochre stain away with my thumb.

Men shovel soil onto the coffin until they tire and the machine takes over.

Turkish Cypriot —Geldi mezarlık dribanı! *Here comes the well digger!*
—Bir o eksikdi. *As if that's all that's missing.*

The coffin is lowered in. We watch as the backhoe dumps the soil and by hand we throw some lumps of mud in ourselves for good measure. My siblings are in a car nearby, they are too young to see this kind of thing. A hoca *Muslim scholar who can lead prayers* is here to pray for my nene's soul but mostly it feels like it's for our benefit. When not praying in Arabic he speaks Turkish. He tells us to stop crying; he said this when we were at the mosque earlier, too.

—God's will, God's decision, this is the way God granted.
—Allahın izni ile. Allahın emri ile. Allah boyle nasıp eti.

The flowers were wasted under the soil, I think. Along with the cheaper carnations, I saw a wreath of white roses cast on top of the coffin then covered with mud. The ones still left on top are zambak, white lilies. They smell strongly. I overhear a couple of old women discussing how you can get rid of the smell of Easter lilies in about five minutes with a pair of tweezers.

—If you tweeze the poleni out of the flower after it's opened you have to be careful, make sure you've got newspaper underneath.
—It doesn't matter, if the pollen gets everywhere I can just tape it off.

There is a man here who my mother has nicknamed 'Topuz Paşa', or 'Prince of the Shepherd Staff'. He got the nickname because he was always threatening to hit someone with a stick. He's in his forties and even though I'm about ten he comments on the way I look a little too much . . .

—She's a pretty one, y'know?"
—I do know, Ali, thank you . . .

These kinds of men turn up out of the blue, making my mother run to the bathroom before she opens the door. She looks in the mirror, frowns and then gets to the front door. When she invites them in, they usually go into the garden, shut the door behind them and chatter while they smoke. She goes through cigarette after cigarette.

When we leave the cemetery, the smell of incense follows us to the car. Once we get in, I pull my headscarf back down to itch at my neck. We're heading back home and all of the cars are following us back.

My mum hasn't taught me how to pray before my first mevlit. The prayer session has made my house busier than I've ever seen it, mostly with people who haven't been over since I was born. They bring semolina helva and other funeral treats. Someone has thrown one tray of helva in the dustbin – it's too soggy. The husbands have been put in the kitchen. The door has been left ajar and they can hear the hoca's mevlit prayer from there. It sounds like he's singing. My headscarf keeps falling off. It smells of mothballs from being stuffed in a drawer for too long. I carry a polished tray around the room to women sat crying on rugs, and splash lemon kolonya on their hands. They rub it on their faces, sighing with relief.

A lady from the local cafe jumps up as soon as the prayers are over to prepare food for the hoca. I join her in the kitchen. Topuz Paşa is standing apart from the other men, frowning at his phone. From the trays I take one of each pastry to a plate and start serving. The hoca leaves early, taking food with him. I hear Panny speaking to someone I don't recognise.

—I'm an old friend of this family, back to Cyprus days. Makbule's husband was a lovely man, died too young. At least they're together now. Poor Ayla, alone with the kids.

I resent my dede in moments like this. He doesn't seem a good enough reason for my nene to be dead. I wonder about some of the last things I heard my nene say about him. I don't know if I heard her right because all I can really think of when I try to picture him is 'fasulye head'.

People start to leave. Zade has offered to take Erhan and İpek to hers for the night but I'm to look after my mother. She's already begun cleaning and I can hear some women saying, how rude to have gone to the sink while they're still walking out. Her hands have foamed up from washing when she comes back to the front door to see people off.

—Nur içinde yatsın *Rest in light*
—Allah rahmet eylesin *Rest in peace*
—Ring us any time you need, Ayla.

Things are quiet again and the house smells of the mevlit. We open all the windows together and sit watching TV. My mum is smoking a lot. She tells me stories about Nene. How she would walk to the mosque in our village through a field of wheat and 'goat's foot weed' to pray for her husband. Or how, when I was born, she would cover me in so much olive oil that I stank. I remind her that it is good that Nene is buried where she is, we picked the best place. Zade told me there is a nearby cemetery where they found human bones: apparently grave robbers are stripping corpses of their valuables, then leaving them out in the open for the families of the dead to find the next day. She tells me she's worried she won't be able to get the government to cover the funeral costs as she's paid for some of it already. Just because she's paid for it doesn't mean she can afford it. As the night sets in we put the kettle on and the sound of it is comforting. We have mint tea and my mum gets a text, explains she's tired and goes to sleep.

—Shut the windows before you come upstairs, annem.

But it's a hot night and there is a breeze to the couch at just the right angle. I radio-surf, stopping on 100.4 FM. Each one is a bop. I fall asleep to garage instrumentals, freestyles in my half dreams:

We take girls from broken homes
Mind yourself!

> *Where's my uzi, where's my phone?*
> *Come on, mate, cook the man some eggs*

blaze it, deface it, I rearrange it

> Shut up, fool . . .
> *wheel up and come again*
> *I don't care who they are, where they are,*
> *if they wanna bring beef here we are.*
> You're gonna wake her up.

I wake up when the music cuts off. Something makes a crashing noise.

When my eyes open, I see these men. I like their trainers. One has a pair of black Nike Pennys on, they look so fresh, you know they had their own shelf back home. They're standing around a small pile that has our TV, DVD player and some bits from my mum's room.

I call for her and get smacked, this big-boy slap around the face. It's the first time I have ever been hit by a man. My mum is walked downstairs, she looks at me and I wonder if she is blaming me. Even I am blaming me. It's warm and they have closed the windows behind them. One of them has nice aftershave on, the one who smacked me. I feel glad Mum fell asleep in her clothes. I think of slasher films and American women who sleep in lingerie running away from your Freddy Kruegers and Jasons.

—Look at her, little mamacita.

Mum looks at me, tells me not to worry and laughs at them. They start shoving at her and she falls, mouth in an Ö, teeth bucking into the floor. They won't let me go to her. It looks like her front tooth has come out. Her hand goes to her face and she stays in a shape, front on the carpet. She's spitting a lot.

—Mind my shoes, man, mind my shoes.

The guy talking is edging away from her cautiously. When she starts shouting in Turkish, one of them understands her.

—You know what, I know this hātūn.^queen She's not alone around here. Come quick.

Ottoman Turkish

They leave through the front door quietly. When I go to her, I have never felt safer. We hug each other on the floor around our pile of things and I close my eyes and can't picture my dad's face.

TURKISH COFFEE, 1999

*Old boy cafe. But in this
context a working men's cafe*

Moruk Kahveci has a sign that says OPEN on its door. It also
has MEMBERS ONLY fixed in rigid plastic above it. It's next
to a Western Union, so you can spot it from a distance because
of the glaring yellow sign adjacent to it. Inside, there are fifteen
men, mostly talking to each other or playing table games.
Some men hold the essential accessory to debate, tesbih.
These are prayer or worry beads that jangle in the air. Some
men use tesbih so they drink less, while some hold the beads
in one hand and drink with the other. In the corner of the
room is a small TV that has the news crackling in the background. One old man fondly watches news of the former
mayor of Istanbul being released from prison six months
earlier than expected. Another smacks the TV on the way
past and calls it corruption. Above the TV there is a picture
of Atatürk. By the door to the toilet, three men are sat together.

Ali has just pulled his finger out of his mouth and is considering. Ufuk is waving a girl away from their table. Mehmet
is admiring his new wingtips. Whenever someone comes over
to go to the toilet, the three pull their chairs closer together
so it regularly sounds like donkeys braying in the cafe. They
are all fairly young, with Ali the oldest, but for a forty-year-
old his beard is embarrassingly patchy. Ufuk is chewing a

61

toothpick. He gave himself a stick 'n' poke tattoo on his hand at the age of eight – the toothpick makes the mermaid on his hand look as though she is holding a spear.

Ali: Beautiful – my gums went numb like I'd been to the dentist.

Something is yanked away from him by Mehmet.

—You should be selling the gogo not using it.

^{cocaine} appears above "gogo"

—Says you. Who brought this to you?

Mehmet: Kurdish boy called Arj. Nearly same age as Ufuk's little Filiz.

He nudges Ufuk suggestively, who raises his hand to him, only half-aware of how naturally it has risen in defence, before talking.

—He's coming back later to talk to us about his Babo.

Ali smiles and runs his hand over his beard.

—Babo Bekir?

Ufuk: Yes. Mehmet's saying Bekir is looking for a good route. Only hard thing for him is getting it past the Bulgarian border. He wants a connect who'll help get it straight from his brother's chicken farm in Mardin. Eighty-kilo game they're playing. We could retire if he brings us in on this.

Ali: I don't want nothing to do with that. Who said I wanted to retire?

Mehmet slaps Ali on the back. He has a softness in his eyes when he waits for a comeback to Ali's response.

Mehmet: I'm saying this could be the job that stops us doing all this little work.

Ufuk: I don't even feel like I can handle one anahtar. *key, for kilo*
Everyone wants to retire on one big deal, that's the problem.

Ali: Eyvallah! *We entrust to God!*

Mehmet: I've got both hands open for it, kardaş.[bro]

Ali: That's why we see you out there on the streets waiting for your *in*, like a player begging for the ball.

Ali imitates Mehmet begging for a ball by putting both his hands together and cocking his head to the side, looking servile. Ufuk interjects:

—Let me tell you a story, moruk.[old bag, old boy, geezer] You go to your English friend's house and he can't stop flirting with his wife, opucuk opucuk—[kissy kissy]

Ali, whose laughter seems to stop at his teeth, cuts him off mid-sentence. At this interruption, Ufuk takes out his tesbih and starts counting them with his fingers until it's quiet again.

Ufuk: Anyway, one person in the room snaps at them, 'go get a room!' and another doesn't look out of respect. But I use my imagination – strip his wife naked in my head and then times her by fifty.

Laughter starts again, from Ali.

Ali: Ne pis adam![What a dirty man!] Admitting you're a pervert?

Ufuk: Don't you see? I get that woman by building you not one but fifty copies of her. I don't need one perfect wife. Or one good deal. I've got my imagination, the work can keep coming. You've got to make lots of deals, keep cloning that success.

Ufuk has confused one of his companions. Mehmet is standing up and stretching to reach a shelf above his head. His pot belly is kept in check by a tight chequered shirt. He can't find what he is looking for and sits back down.

Ali: You think you're building an empire in this business, Ufuk?

Turkish Cypriot

63

Ufuk: Not an empire. I am building, yes. For my family. I don't want Filiz going to that NPK school forever, but I will bring my money in bit by bit.

Mehmet: Take her out of school then! I don't know, Ufuk... Every Turk comes along thinking he's a family man as though he hasn't already failed at the family business and given up his daytime job for quick money.

Mehmet puts his hand up for a moment. He walks over to an empty table and takes a brown board from the table. He returns with it tucked under his arm and cocks his head to the side, waiting for Ufuk's response.

Ufuk: I am everyone's family man. You come to me, I'll be exactly here in twenty years' time looking after my own. Damla damla göl olur. *Drop by drop makes a lake*

Mehmet: You think too small. How can your kids learn anything from a man who's happy to eat hamsi *anchovy* for a living? You see me. I'm going to be drinking bottles of champagne with eight grams of gogo in them. Do things with big style.

He smacks a backgammon board down on the table before brushing residual bits of tobacco from it. It seems almost sweaty from his armpit.

Mehmet: If you played more tavla, you would get places faster.

An OK hand gesture is made in response. Mehmet smiles. He has black-capped teeth. They open the board and start setting it up. Mehmet's fingers reverently slide six of the chequers into place, while Ufuk piles them in his hand and starts whacking them down in lines on the board. Ali speaks to them while they play:

—Neyse, *anyway* I had a nice girly come to me with something. She's got a lot of gear because her boyfriend's been put away, so she wants to share her portion with me if I do the admin.

Mehmet: What, so you do the meet and greet for her boyfriend? I'm not getting it. What for?

Ufuk: Şeş! *Six!*

A double six is thrown and Mehmet groans, concentrating more on the game than on the conversation.

Farsi numbers are used in tavla

Ali: She knows what's what. She had me making her çay *tea* while she put down the blueprints, but she's a bit too ready to trust.

Ufuk: Sometimes people want it done fast. Did she look pregnant to you?

Ali: No. She's been got with kids already. Three of them actually! She had this oldness to her . . . body young, though.

A six and a one are rolled. Ufuk loses his lead to Mehmet, who has perked up.

Mehmet: Sounds great, can I help her too?

Ali: You have to find out who her boyfriend is first.

Ufuk: Who?

Ali: He's opened up the shop off Lordship Lane, Nehir.

Mehmet: Who's watching it now?

Ali: He's got his neighbour Sadi in there. Old one. My plan is that we help her with this but, same time, one of us goes to this place to make sure he's settled in and bring him in with the others.

Mehmet: I can go tomorrow.

TOMORROW

Nehir supermarket has been named after a river. The vegetables are old in the shopfront but inside, you can get a packet
of twenty cigarettes for £1.50. Under the counter, of course.
Everything you buy has a film of dust on it. If you buy crisps,
they are squashed pieces already. On this day, an old man is
sat on a stool behind the counter, eating spiced pickles out
of a jar. His moustache seems to hang apart from his face,
stiff as though sprayed with setting spray. A stocky man in
a leather coat interrupts him. This man is about thirty and
because of a childhood injury he has a smile that starts with
his right nostril, which makes his face look like it's been
whacked into place with a shovel.

   —Naber, beyefendi? *What's up, my gentleman?*

   —Welcome, welcome.

   —What's your name, my friend?

   —Sadi, like my father.

   —My name's Mehmet. My family owns the shop opposite.

   —Really? I've been over to introduce myself, they didn't
mention they had a son.

   —They do have a son – five, actually. We're a big family.

   —Well, I'm happy to meet you, don't be a stranger. Funnily,

I asked your parents over to mine already, have a meal with us this Saturday.

—We can all go together, maybe. Where do you live?

—Please, you're all welcome. Hepiniz. *All of you* We are just off here, actually, Elsden. I'll write it before you go. Can I get you anything today, grab something from the fridge?

—Thank you.

A can of Mirinda is opened. Mehmet's beard bobbing with each glug.

—You know, some people have no hospitality left in them.

—Ach, it's nothing, honestly. This place is almost like my son's business, I watch it for my neighbour. Good man. He wouldn't want a friend thirsty.

—Well, you're good to your neighbours, this kindness will return to you.

—A Muslim doesn't do one thing to get one thing back.

—Yes, but I can give you something back for a small piece. My business partners and me look after every shop in this area. Çok az gibi. *Such a little* You must know about us. We look after each other. Down the road, you have the cake shop, Amed – they help us too. It's tax.

Something like amusement shows in Sadi's face. There's a bit of pickled carrot stuck on his front tooth. The pickle jar, however, has been put away, at some moment between 'for a small piece' and 'us'.

—It's a dangerous area, kardaş, *Bro* some of the businesses around here only look out for their own. You've got these gangs going after that young boy in the cafe down the road last week. Did you see the amount of traffic when they got him? So many people trying to drive close so they could spot a friend in the crowd.

Mehmet places his can in the bin by Sadi's feet. He comes eye to eye with Sadi's slippers, wet on the bottom from being worn outside. He has small feet.

—Anyway, I see you're a family man. Well, my friends are all in this by blood, not by party tricks. You either go with us or you go with someone else. Nobody stays here for long on their own. Pay us ten per cent of what you make and we'll be fine.

—I'm not on my own. If you come back here, my own wife could run you off. You spend so long looking at people's feet that you don't check their hands.

A sawn-off shotgun is propped under the counter. Sadi's aim is fixed anywhere between Mehmet's waist and his breastbone.

—Don't you care I had enough respect to come empty-handed?

—Just go.

—I'll see you when we come to eat. Elsden Road is it?

—Hoşçakal.^{Bye} If you come it will be to kiss my hand sorry.

POKER AND CHEETOS

In Moruk Kahveci, if anyone wants a tea they can ask Agata, who is there most days. She used to date Mehmet until his gogo habit made him too paranoid to be with a cafe girl. There was something exciting to her about being allowed into this netted room. She didn't want him to take her out of this life and put her neatly somewhere else. Every man in this space was well dressed and they knew their etiquette. They all rolled up like they were salting a leg of lamb, lovingly and with precision. Even the way they played poker. It took a lot to make them shout. You could first tell when they were angry from under the table, some of the men gripped their thighs so tight you could see their knuckles change colour or they would take their tesbih out. Mehmet always drummed on the table when he got agitated. Something that sounded to her like the Arsenal club song. She knew that was because he liked people to see if he was annoyed.

Mehmet: I've been folding all these times and I folded my way up to four. I mean I can't do no better than four unless I win the next hand.

Suddenly you hear a collective grumble. The game comes to a quick end.

Mehmet: Where's your aces now then? This is what I'm teaching you, this is the art of folding!

Player 1: Don't give us any more of your therapy, Mehmet. Vay be, vay be. *Oh my days*

One of the men around the table tosses his tissue on the table and gets up to go to the toilet. Mehmet shakes his head while throwing one hand in the air in front of himself.

—Allah Allah, *Literally: God, God. Here: bloody hell* it's as though I've killed your family the way you're going on.

The TV in the background has been turned up and it seems like this bit of the day is coming to an end. Agata brings coffee over. She has taken the crema off the top of one of them to bring to a man who is sat apart from the others, watching TV. He is waiting to see what the man playing poker for him wins. They split their costs because he finds it stressful playing himself. Everyone treats him with respect, bowing their heads when he enters the room. An octogenarian, he has a very large head and fat that pokes through his shirt buttons until the buttons seem to siphon off his blood supply. Agata finds him disconcerting. He does barely any talking unless something happens on the TV.

—İnanmıyorum! *I can't believe it!*

Yusuf is outraged that the Cheetos mouse has been replaced with Chester Cheetah. Chester's voice (also the voice of the well-loved voice actor Fatih Özacun) reminds him of a man who cheated him once. Last time he complained about this, someone replied how a Turkish marketing person imagined Chester and, therefore, the community should take pride in him. On that day, he was so wound up that he took his coat off his chair and shuffled out of the cafe.

Mehmet: Yusuf Bey, I've just got a few shearlings in. Sheepskin. Ajda, can you try this one on for me? Look look look at how it looks on her.

Mehmet shoves the shearling coat onto Ajda/Agata, who struggles to pull her arms through, the sheepskin a stark white against her black striped apron.

Mehmet: Are you sure you're not a size 12?

Agata takes the jacket off and drapes it over the back of Yusuf's chair.

Mehmet: Doesn't suit you, stuff like that, anyway! Don't know why I bother . . . Anyway, Yusuf abi, this is what we have for today. I didn't win anything else on the poker table. I'll bring you more bits soon. *for God's sake!*

Yusuf: That's no good, Allah aşkına! Mehmet, I've got a poem for you, watch me:

Ben sana bok demem,	I won't call you a shit,
Boklar duyar ar eder.	The shit would feel bad.
Bir zerren düşse boka,	If a piece of you fell in shit,
Onu da mundar eder.	It would spoil the shit.
Tanrı senin hamurunu	At creation you were dough
Necasetle yoğurmuş,	Kneaded with shit,
Anan seni sıçar iken	Your mother gave birth to you accidentally
Yanlışlıkla doğurmuş.	While shitting.

Mehmet: Yusuf abi, I understand you. My mind is your mind. I'll bring you more fast, not soon. You know how it is.

During this exchange, Ali has walked into the cafe. He doesn't look Yusuf in the eye when he reaches the two and instead bows his head respectfully.

Ali: Yusuf dayı, you have the best memory in this room. Fancy you knowing that entire poem.

Yusuf: Ali, some of us have etiquette. We know what we should know and do what we should do. At this exact moment the world has a million Mehmets but only one me, still he acts pislik gibi. *like a piece of shit*

Yusuf gets a nod from Ali for this.

Ali: Well, we have a lot to learn from you. What's that you're watching in the background?

Yusuf: Nothing, just a bit of Kemal Sunal—

Yusuf's attention turns to the TV, where *Tosun Paşa* is on the screen. Kemal Sunal is struggling in a hammam as a man tips scalding water on him. Ali taps Mehmet on the shoulder once and sits himself in the corner. Mehmet waits a minute for Yusuf's laughter to kick in then comes over.

Mehmet: He had me with a gun.

Ali: Memo, you mean you got had with a gun by an old man.

Mehmet (shrill fluctuations): It's annoying! Now Ufuk's wife is down his neck because she knows Sadi's wife Pembe and she's embarrassed she can't go there for dinner. Can you imagine?

Ali: Give it a bit and then send the English boys. He lives on Elsden Road, two minutes away, really.

Ali has gestured towards Agata to come over. She walks past the TV screen – momentarily blocking the screen – before reaching their table.

Yusuf, from behind: Watch it, woman!

Agata: Sorry, sorry . . . Good to see you, Ali. Have you sorted our friend out yet? He just told me I'm fat.

Ali: What's that idiot's opinion to you anyway?

He laughs. Mehmet has started to roll his Rizla, tobacco has scattered over the table.

Ali: Tovbe tovbe, *Mercy, mercy* you're getting it everywhere.

Mehmet: How much patience do you think I have with you two taking the piss, you keep all jumping on my head . . . I'm not a trampoline!

Neither Agata nor Ali look to him as he says this.

Ali: Agata, have you seen Ufuk today? I want a tea if you don't mind.

Ali passes her a tip across the table, wiping off the tobacco as he does so. Agata takes it and puts it in the large front pocket of her combat trousers.

Agata: I did, but he rushed off because his daughter got into some trouble on the way to school. Didn't he ring you?

Ali: No, his phone's off.

Mehmet: I told him to take Filiz out of that school, didn't I?

Agata: No, you told him to take her out of school. That's different.

Mehmet: It didn't happen at her school, it happened on the way to school. Nothing too big, I think she just battered a girl. Duğmuş bir kızı. *Literally: batterer girl. Meaning, girl who likes a fight*

Ali frowns before he speaks.

Ali: Can't see why he'd get so angry about that. I don't believe that for one second.

Mehmet: Can I have a tea too, please, Ajda?

Agata tuts then heads to a small kitchenette at the back of the cafe. Mehmet leans towards Ali; he's lit his roll-up and puts it to his mouth.

Ali: Looks like you've got more on your plate than this shop stuff, take this and get it to Yusuf, it came in from the other day.

A small bag gets tossed across the table towards Mehmet. Mehmet's smile is all on the right side of his face, gap-toothy, smoke escapes through his teeth.

FOLLOWING UP ON ALI'S
SUGGESTION, 1999

A moustache touches the pavement. Two hands speckled with age spots are pressed on the ground in front of the moustache. Sadi's wife Pembe starts to run out from her house towards the children who have her husband like that. She gets stopped by one boy on a bike who cycles right up to her face. They all seem to have identical hair, lank and greasily twisted behind their ears.

—Tell her to forget us too or she'll be riding empty buses standing by the time I'm done with her!

Pembe knows to leave her husband outside would hurt him less than joining him there.

—You joker, you're disgusting, look how old she is.

—Are you blind, bruv? Old as he is. Fool!

Before they leave one of them tosses a brick through her window. This is Pembe's first incident of violence since arriving in London twenty years ago; like she was told about.

EDGE OF THE BED MEHMET,
ONE WEEK LATER

Agata lives near Moruk cafe in a shared house. She is an efficient person to live with. Every winter she will be the first to ring her landlord when — and not if — the boiler is not working, even if it is 3 a.m. She labels her food. AGATA. Written across her cheese (almost always smoked) and her kabanos. She eats from a pack of them every night before dinner, and measures what goes back in carefully because some of her housemates think the sausages taste just like Peperami. On depression days, she wears them on her wrist like a bracelet and eats at them while in bed. Her house is close to a shop where she gets herself warm bread in the morning. She tests the bread carefully, knocking its underside and prodding until she has found the one she likes. If it isn't good enough, she gets Mother's Pride. Her room is on the ground floor, it is noisy at night but she is the closest to a toilet, which is right outside her room and also noisy at all hours. She has a single bed, a chest of drawers and a bucket where she keeps her toiletries. Propped against her window is a corkboard, where she pins photos and flyers. Some of the flyers are for protests, *Love music hate racism*, and one on the London Eye. She is sat on her bed, and has offered a chair from the kitchen to Mehmet, who is sitting with his head between his knees.

Agata: Tied her up! Why would he do that to his own daughter?

Mehmet lifts his head up and looks up at Agata, almost in disbelief. As though he realises for the first time that he has been speaking to her.

Mehmet: I didn't see it myself. Maybe if he's strict on her, his other little one, Cemile, will know not to do what she does. He thinks if he disciplines her like this that she'll change, change to what I don't know. She's been seeing someone right in front of his nose.

Agata: Blows my head how her mum lets that happen.

Mehmet has let out his belt, the popcorn sound of it slowly releasing his belly. He has started to doze off. Agata covers him with a blanket, and then watches him from the edge of her bed. Two of her housemates have just slammed the front door shut; the sound of their talking fades as they climb the stairs.

FILIZ WASN'T ACTUALLY IN BUGSY MALONE

Two weeks on there are no signs of the ligatures that bound Filiz. He had left her trussed up as a lesson, long enough for her pride and feet to turn near purple. The room where this took place was in the spare bedroom upstairs, the room where her little sister Cemile now plays. Filiz's dad has come to sit next to her on the couch. On the TV screen there is a wedding, where Halay dancers are forming a circle. Above their heads are framed photos of the family. Two generations behind Ufuk, his great-grandfather stands out from all the photos for his fez-and-woollen-waistcoat-with-suit combo. Another photo, much newer, is one of Filiz. She is thirteen, in a school photo with Clara Bow eyebrows and a matte brown lipstick that she thought made her look like Aaliyah. Ufuk has turned the channel from what Filiz was watching to the same TV show he had watched the night before. They sit in silence until Filiz's mother walks in.

—We've got guests coming. Filiz, will you help me carry the chairs in here?

Filiz jumps up and walks into the kitchen with her mum. In between the cooker and a counter is a gap where some folded wooden chairs are wedged. She goes to pull one out.

Filiz: He's watching the same thing again as though he couldn't just leave the TV on *Deli Yürek*.

Tulay (whispering): He likes to watch again in case he misses something. Sakin ol. *Calm down* You know he doesn't like to watch that racist show either.

Filiz: Like he's so perfect. I only watch it for Kenan.

Tulay: Don't think he won't know that.

The conversation pauses while they carry two chairs each through to the living room. Ufuk is laughing at what he's watching. They walk back into the kitchen.

Filiz: You forget the decade we're in sometimes, I swear.

Tulay: Shhh, before your dad hears you, so we can try and make it into a new one.

Tulay climbs up onto the counter with a sock over her hand. She then uses her socked hand to wipe the walls and catch dust. Filiz loosens one of her mum's slippers so it hangs precariously from her foot.

Tulay: What are you, Cemile's age? Put that back.

The slipper has dropped off onto the floor, and Tulay's stockinged bunions reveal themselves. They both laugh in their throats. Hum hum hum types of laughs.

Filiz: Hope you have the heating on.

Tulay: I'll put it on half an hour before your nene gets here. When your deyze *auntie on your mum's side* brings her she gets hot in the car. It doesn't need to be too stuffy in here. *Turkish Cypriot*

Filiz starts to throw decorative towels over the cutlery inside the drawer and stow away any evidence of cleaning supplies.

Tulay: Quickly wipe under the washing machine, the lino has gone all white from when you dropped the powder.

Filiz: Isn't this enough now? I need to go and change before they get here.

Tulay: Who's coming that you have to change for?

A slipper slides slowly back onto Tulay's foot. Filiz offers her mum a hand to get down from the counter.

Filiz: You can get a cheap step from the shop by West Green Road. If you give me money I'll get you one on the walk home.

Tulay: Your dad is picking you up from school this week. Go with him and he'll pay for it.

They walk back into the living room and put a couple of bowls down on the coffee table. Ufuk takes some nuts from the bowl closest to him.

Filiz: Baba,^Dad can we go to the bric-a-brac shop on the way back tomorrow?

Tulay: No, not West Green Road, go with your mum somewhere else next week.

Filiz: I can go alone tomorrow and you can get me on Tuesday instead.

Ufuk: What's this attitude? First your school says they find you kissing on the stage and now you act like last week never happened. Telling me you're doing *Bugsy Malone*. Is that what you call drama?

Ufuk turns and looks towards Tulay. He raises his hands up in the air as though he is announcing himself. Tulay puts her hand on Filiz's shoulder.

Ufuk: Telling me you're doing *Bugsy Malone*.

Filiz: It was three weeks ago, actually.

Ufuk: Kes sessini!   *Cut your noise!*

Tulay steps in front of her daughter before turning to her.

Tulay: Filiz, go upstairs with Cemile, you need to help her pick something to wear.

A head of curly hair peeps from the doorway. Filiz starts leaving the room. Her dad's voice rises behind her.

Ufuk: If I could have found that boy I would have shot his dad!

Tulay places her hand on the arm of the couch, as close as she wants to get.

Tulay: She's gone, canım.   *my life*   Don't let your children wind you up. Things are good. When your daughters start to hate you, that's when the whole world hates you.

Ufuk: You don't hate me, do you?

She squeezes his arm firmly. The volume of the TV goes up. When she walks to the bedroom upstairs, she finds Filiz brushing Cemile's hair so roughly it pulls at the skin on her forehead. Looking at the carpet stretched out ahead of her, lint seems to be appearing out of the blue. Small curls at her feet making themselves known.

Tulay: Go wet a sponge so you can pick those bits up.

Filiz: I don't want to walk past him.

Tulay: It's fine. I'll finish Cemile's hair. You should have used a comb. Just go straight to the kitchen and come back, no problem.

BABO, MAYBE A FEW WEEKS AFTER, STILL 1999 (IT'S BEEN A LONG YEAR)

Five minutes from a Sainsbury's and just past a bric-a-brac shop is a terrace house on a corner. It has blackout curtains in the front. When you walk in, the staircase in front leads up to a soundproof, three-inch-thick door. If invited through there, the first thing you might spot would be the three large black metal hooks screwed into the ceiling. They hang there like little fingers, crooked and beckoning. Elsewhere, live electrics are visible. Some comfortable chairs. At this moment the room is empty. A cup of tea has been left on a dining chair in the centre of the room; a fly rests on the cup.

Downstairs a man sits under many blankets at his couch. His feet are up on a lace puff puff. Clean, nail-filed old man toes. Through the blankets a lump is moving. It goes from between his legs and up past his stomach before emerging. The cat is a fat little thing. She comes up to his nose before pawing him in the face. He picks her up by the belly and puts her behind him, rerouting the cat so she walks along the headrest and then stops to look at the waterfall installation. Or, more specifically, the Lighted Moving Motion Waterfall Mirror with Nature Sounds – bought for £40 at an Algerian supermarket near Finsbury Park. Within a thick silver frame, the waterfall ripples softly. Inchingly. The leaves on the mopane trees that dwarf the water are fixed, a pixelated forest of them. The cat is watching. Keeps watching until she starts to lick under her nails. When a cuckoo starts on with its hollow sound, she lifts her head to watch again. Coo-coo-coo. Her ears flatten. Then a hummingbird. Then the Asian Koel, whose cry sounds like it is yelling 'I will!' And back again; in a continuous cycle until eventually the cat tries to attack.

Disturbed by the commotion, the man takes his hands out from a packet of salted sunflower seeds and swats her from the couch, but it is too late, she has already disturbed the frame. It shakes threateningly above the couch. A raven caws. The cat has fluffed out and darts out of the room before a newspaper is thrown her way. Standing up, the man straightens the frame. He is a tall man who looks like a melted bottle of cola; the space between his man boobs and muffin top extends Mr Blobby-style. As he goes to sit back down, the door rings in a repeating triplet beat, the breaks long enough for the pattern to stand out. He puts his slippers on and goes to the door, where he is asked to open his garden door. He does. Through the back door, a man with a bedcover thrown over him is led into the house. There is no muffled screaming, just acceptance.

The man under the bedcover has been working at the back of a pound shop, selling skunk behind a short wall to teenagers and people who are OK with getting bumped. Two weeks after this moment, the shop will be burnt down in an arson attack. The only casualty from the fire: a lovebird stuck in its cage for one week after its owner died. A shame. The art of getting rid of someone disrespectful (this man, one of many faceless men) is very similar to burning a building for insurance money. It's an anonymous activity that starts with setting a spark off in one place. Little metal fingers (crooked, beckoning) remain latched onto the man's collar; a fly circles, disturbed by the swinging. What the man did is irrelevant now, and dealt with.

TWO WEEKS AFTER
BEDCOVER MAN INTERRUPTS
BABO AND HIS CAT

There are two cafes on Factory Road. Both are run by the same people but with different priorities. Both have shutters down and cameras on the door. Before getting to the door, people wanting to come in need to call. One of them is an old kahveci *coffee shop* that has been shut down. From the street it looks like what it is. Even a fourteen-year-old would have a reasonable expectation of what to find inside. The lighting within is dark as dishwater. In the middle of the room is a pool table, the felt cover ruched up around the edges. Around it are mismatched chairs: folded deckchairs, school chairs, dining chairs and armchairs. At the back of the room there's a gap in the wall – a window to another room, with no glass. If you stand at this windowless window you can ask for as little as a £5 bag of weed. If you get that far into the room, you can see through to a kitchen where a woman is making coffee, crema and all. By a fruit machine in the corner, a man sits reading. His hair touches the shoulders of his pleather bomber jacket, a jacket complemented by baggy boot-cut jeans and TNs almost totally covered by the hem of his trousers. A man walks into the room. He is about sixty, has an Einstein head of hair and a melting cola-bottle body. When Babo speaks, it comes out sweetly.

Kurmanji (Kurdish)

Chief, boss. Respectful term for someone who has a fatherly effect upon people

Turkish, from Arabic

Babo: Selam. *Hello* Where is Arjîn?

Arjîn gets up from his chair and kisses Melted Cola Bottle man on his hand.

Kurmanji

Arjîn: Selam, ba kheir bît. *May you have come without sorrows. Meaning 'welcome'* I would have come to your house, you didn't have to come all the way here, abi. How's your back?

Babo: It's OK. You know, if I act like it's been run over once, you all think I have ten cars on my back every day.

Arjîn: You deserve to rest though, always working so hard.

Babo (with annoyance): It seems to me that I lose money when I rest, Arjîn. Enough with this treating me like I'm dying.

Arjîn: Sorry.

Babo can hear Arjîn scratching at his index nail with his thumbnail. It sounds like a wooden güiro being scraped by a stick.

After a silence:

Arjîn: Have you heard about that Cypriot girl that's trying to work with Ali? Her boyfriend didn't come back after he bought from us and now he's in jail, five years.

Babo: How long is she saying she'll take to sell it?

Arjîn: It's not important. She seems like she has a plan. Sometimes we have to look beneath our feet, not over our heads.

Babo: Or behind your back before they pull the rug out from beneath your feet. Check in on her, speed things up.

Arjîn: I will. Have you heard of our guy caught body packing coming out of Bosnia? I saw on the news this Kellaway English man who thinks the NIS *National Identification Service, a department of London Metropolitan Police* know their left from their right.

Their chat is interrupted by two teenage girls. One walks in. She has big curly hair. _{Brother. Term of respect}

—Hello, is Arjîn abi here?

—He's in the corner. Busy.

Arjîn excuses himself to Babo and walks to the middle of the room.

—Don't abi me, Filiz, nice to have you back.

He chucks four different bags of weed on the pool table.

—Pick which one you like.

Filiz gives the type of smile she saves for when a man makes her feel special. Same look she gives her dad coming back from work with a crate of fruit.

—That one.

—That'll be the same again . . .

He hears the smack on his head before the pain reaches him and turns in shock to Babo, who is addressing the girls.

Babo: Whose daughter are you two babies?

—No one you know.

—My dad travels selling fruit for his job, you might see him on Lordship Lane sometimes.

The room starts to tickle with laughter. Babo tries to lean towards her, his body big, it seems like he could topple.

Babo: Ufuk's daughter? Come here, let me look at you.

Filiz moves away from her friend. She is wearing hoops with her school uniform so when she lifts her chin up to look in his eyes, the hoops shake.

Babo (to Arjîn): Give this one free.

CHASING, NEXT DAY

On top of a bric-a-brac shop, a needle hangs out of a vein. A needle hangs out of another vein on another arm. One girl is sleeping and has left the needle in. She has been out for hours. One needle girl smiles at a man who is fixated upon her as he injects her blood back into her. Flushback. First, the blood comes out, then a push and it returns. These women have made £50 to £100 today on a job. There are about fifteen of them who have brought their earnings here. A lot of them wear pyjamas or jogging bottoms and have set themselves up for a home-away-from-home day.

A girl hands another a tube made out of foil. A little black spot on the foil starts turning into liquid tar. It starts running down. Through the tube she tries to suck at all the smoke, chasing the dragon in its twists and turns.

—You wanna come down? Here, take a few lines of this.

Mehmet keeps photos of his loved ones around this flat. Ufuk with Tulay and his two daughters. One of Ali when he was little. He has blown up a huge photo of Agata's niece, who is his god-daughter, even though he told them he doesn't believe in all that and barely made it to her christening.

In his bedroom, he has opened a drawer and he looks at

the money in front of him. It's about eight thousand, which is just this week's profit.

He had a shape up on his beard recently but the scar stretching from his chin to his nose still makes his entire face look wonky. Agata always said it gave him character. It cheapens his ex when she compliments him because it reminds him of the other types of cafe girls – like the ones in the cafe near his flat. On his bed are two empty tubs of cutting agent: baby laxative and white sugar. He has been making more out of his gear.

Before leaving, he rolls up one of the notes in front of him and taps at his bedside table before leaning over. When he comes up, he holds his palm between his eyebrows, as though he has had bad news. Out the house. Before he stops off at Cafe Two, he stands in the queue of a McDonald's until someone comes and claps him on the back, holds him hug tight and swaps one Tesco bag for another before announcing he's got to rush back to his son in the car.

CAFE TWO, SAME DAY

Cafe Two on Factory Road is busy. It can be entered from a back alleyway that is otherwise reserved for a row of garages where residents keep their cars. Near this strip there's a Greek restaurant, a hairdresser's and a Greek Cypriot grocer's that supplies the restaurant with lounza sausage. A couple of the girls who waitress at Cafe Two are at Mehmet's. They only work outside the cafe if they need to top up their wages on dates with men who come to the cafe. The men with the driest chat mysteriously end up with the chattiest and liveliest women. They flirt by asking the girls, 'How would you feel if I didn't pay you?' Sometimes they are girls from mainland Turkey, or Romanian girls who speak Turkish with an American accent. Black Sea girls and Danube girls. While the men play cards they brush their breasts on them. They have a different vibe from other coffee girls, you can tell by how often the coffee is burnt at the stove. It isn't that they can't do it. It's that they don't like the men they make it for. They don't have to like someone to tell them 'Ay yavrım, buyuk daşaklım!' *Oh, my very existence, big-balled man of mine!*

Turkish Cypriot

—You've got nothing to go home to, you give this up, you're giving up your family . . .

—Sounds like you're talking about yourself.

—Got happy slapped in a snooker hall!

—Should have dashed the snooker ball in his eye.

—Tells me she's emigrating to Australia now she's made up her money.

—Eve gelince, bir arkadaşla gelecem.

The conversations lump together. Amidst it all, Mehmet is telling a story to Babo.

Mehmet: So Ali has gone to this girl and she thinks she's got coke to get rid of. He's saying, 'Like fuck it's coke, I know when heroin is heroin.' He starts running it. He picks up the foil, starts burning it, making it run all over the foil. 'What the fuck, man,' he goes, 'you know this stuff is pure, there's not even a speck of dirt in here.'

Babo keeps his face closed.

Mehmet: I thought I'd speak to you personally. We're the ones helping her. So I know about your brother and the chickens.

Babo: That's done now, we need another way.

Mehmet: I can help you with that. This girl has come to us with this idea about cabbages. Cabbages, cauliflower, broccoli. I don't care what's what. She just put the idea in my head. You haven't got your brother, let me help you. Tabiki canim feda bu ise. *I'd give my life to this*

Mehmet waves casually at a girl across the room.

Babo: Eh? You're going to get in a truck full of lahana and *cabbage* drive it to me from Turkey? And what does your big boss think of this? Look at you, you don't even have enough concentration to have one conversation about this.

Mehmet: No, but Ali can drive it. Everything will run smooth as a baby's head.

Babo: Have Ali come, have Ufuk come. If you come as a three then I've got you. Just one, this is not what I call help.

Mehmet's attention turns to another conversation.

—We made a little foil, we're smoking away, I'm buzzing nicely, cousin's buzzing nicely and then suddenly the door tuck tuck tuck tuck.

—Who was it?

—It was the Greek guy.

—The lorry driver?

—No, no, no. Panny, the old one. Cypriot. Has that beautiful Turkish girl over helping him sometimes. You know, the one with the big tits.

—What? He asking for his rent again?

A crumpling sound. Babo looks at Mehmet, who passes him a roll-up.

Mehmet: One for the road. I'll come back with Ali definitely. Ufuk's been having trouble with his daughter, rumours swinging like monkeys in his ears.

Babo: Filiz? Beautiful girls he has.

They both stand, the eldest getting up first. Mehmet grabs Babo's jacket for him. Then puts his own on.

Babo: Tamam,^{OK} look after yourself.

Mehmet waits for Babo to leave before turning to the boys talking behind him, and then he smacks one of them. His eyes seem electrified by the excitement of getting to smack someone.

Mehmet: Pay your rent, your landlord knows me.

BABO

Not everything is about respect, what people forget is responsibility. Somebody is going to do this, so if you're telling me it's me, then OK, I can do it well. Actually no one is telling me it's me, I came here and I said this is going to have to be what I do. My brother had everyone's respect. I tell you, he walks onto a farm and the chickens go quiet. He's different from me, he's counting the red top bottles, he's got his chemicals in and is hiding them in the dirt. He comes out of jail and starts breeding chicks, telling people he's in the Kurdish Fried Chicken industry. Then he starts digging tunnels like a cird, *black rat. Pest* 'nip, nip', and he's got his little workers going *Kurmanji* at the soil, making this business in the ground, stashing-moving eroîn *heroin*. Now he has gone and got himself arrested, *Kurmanji* and our family name is all over the *Daily Sabah*. We have all this stuff to move. It's made its way through the Golden Crescent and yet now there's no way to do it.

When I was little I lived with nothing in Mêrdîn. My mother used to put me next to the sobah *wood stove* in the middle of the room, I would get nearly as hot as the çay pot boiling inside it. She had a long grey plait and it was as if she had lived sixty years, not forty. I would hold the plait like a donkey tail I was following through a mountain, and sit in front of her as she told me stories. She had a glow in her cheeks, she spoke so much. She told me the story of Gulkhandaran's Flower. There's this perî *genie, fairy, nymph,* who falls in love with a boy. She loves him so much, *cf. cin, ifrit* every time she sees him she laughs and jewels come out her mouth. The boy gifts his king these jewels. The king, of course, tries to kill him because he is getting too rich. His adviser comes up with these plans. Everything from sending him to a demon's mountain, to pushing him into a bonfire, so he can reach his hell. Every single time, the perî saves her lover with magic and allows him to survive the flames. The king is jealous and wants immortality for himself, so he jumps into the fire too. His whole kingdom watches him burn to death.

If I am the king here, my lesson comes like this: let people come up around you. They call me Babo, but I have earned this word from the love that comes with it. When I was little I lived with nothing. Nothing. I'm a tired person. I know that. I know that about myself! They say you have to be organised to run an empire like this. Probably, maybe, I would have had less realpolitik. My men have taken up the pavements. They walk in gangs of ten with their legs out wide and don't care if anyone sees them. You've got them walking on the High Street as if they are all little kings. Next thing they'll start walking around with their arms out of their sleeves, wearing their blazers like a Batman cape. Six men come out of one car to make one drop off. It's clear to me that this is a type of acting, a front, they put themselves everywhere and I am left to cover it. I want my men to do this though. I feel like I am a sack of potatoes – and wherever one potato falls out another potato springs up. The more we spread out, the more mini-mes pop out of the ground. Fake leaders start to crop up everywhere, and they don't handle their business the way I do, and now the shopkeepers want to know me, they even prefer me. You have to pick your poison. If I took out a map of this area, I could put a pin down in a lot of the shops, and a majority of those shops called for me to charge them. Do you know what that means? It means that my men can get away with acting like superstars.

There are other people who work on the same things but to them it's all about power, they've got no love from their people. Especially with the eroîn and the ones who can't get enough of powder power. They make their customers wait. These customers are desperate, they'd do anything, money is nothing, if you haven't got the eroîn, you're nothing. The price goes up the more they go 'Yeah, man, just wait'. What I do, I chuck a few samples just to keep them calm before I sell to them. The dealer I've just sold bulk to says, 'What you doing, you're taking my business – I'm losing a couple hundred quid!' But this is where the love comes from. I've got stash houses everywhere; I've got my main ones, my fake ones. Whenever the smackheads get picked up, they tell the police exactly where I work from and keep stuff. But here's what matters, I always get the message before they arrive. Nobody really grasses. I get someone to clear the place, and things keep running along. They can't stop. This is where the love comes in.

Now the chicken hustle is done and brother's got himself away, it's good to have people come to us with ideas. Everything clever starts with conversation. Have you heard of the Japanese bush warbler? They're island birds. On a small bit of island you have less birds so they don't need complicated song to communicate with each other. They just have this clear signal and know each other. The sound is like a submarine bouncing off another submarine. The ideas man and me. If we speak plain and clear with each other then we're two birds on a small island, no fancy song.

A LESSON FROM ALI,
OCTOBER 1999

Ayla is cleaning her windows today. With one hand she holds up the sill, with the other she pours vinegar into the corners of the ledge. There has been an ant infestation and the fountainhead is here, in a section of broken wood. Her hand is chafed by the sill. As she often does, she wonders how much it would cost to get bay windows fitted, just like all the other Georgian builds off this part of Tottenham High Street. Her children are in the garden; they're following Damla around as she overwaters the plants. A patchy beard comes towards her home. He crosses the road in one straight line and without rerouting lifts his leg over the brick wall banking off her patio. Ayla pulls the window down, crushing some ants in the process. He keeps coming at her until he puts his nose to the glass. There's a delay in the time it takes for his breath to mist it up.

Ali: Napan hanım effendi? *What's up, dear madame?*

Ayla puts her finger to his nose on the glass until it is the only clear spot in a wide circle of fogged-up window and then raises it. One minute. When she opens the door, he has already unlaced his trainers.

Ayla: I wasn't expecting guests.

Ali: Where's your family?

Ayla: They're all in the garden with my mum. Hope this is a quick one, Ali.

Her settee has a doll's arm sticking out of it. Ali pushes it further down into the side of the cushion and they sit facing each other.

Ayla: I'd offer you a drink but the minute they spot me at the sink I'll need to go out in the garden. Just about managed to scare them off by saying we have poisonous ants starting a war next to the TV.

A straight face.

Ali: Funny. So we have three things we're going to do. I send your gear to Jersey, the rest we'll sell off to this Jamaican dealer I know – all very street level – and then I send leftovers to some posh houses near Muswell Hill or something. Full of university people. You don't want everything going off to one place if you want this to be quiet.

Ayla: Jersey?

Ali: Yes. Taking the stuff to Jersey is worth three times more. Little bags worth three thousand sell for seven thousand. Once you've gotten someone on board, the hundred miles there are no problems. There's about a hundred users in the place, so police know when there's stuff on the island. You can spook them with a boo, though. Their prisons are full of non-islanders.

Ayla: They can't fit more than a hundred in one of their prisons?

Ali: Something like that.

Ayla: Bir sey degil. *That's nothing* We're in and out. I've heard that island is full of witches' cats with six toes on each foot.

Laughter kisses through his teeth. When Ali laughs like this, you can see a gold tooth where his incisor should be.

Ali: When was the last time you stopped to double-check a cat's toes? So if you want Jersey, you need start-up money, it takes about a thousand to get a girl to deliver it for you and I want half of what you make. You've got two anahtar *kilos* here. You can't get rid of all of it there. We do a few jobs. The rest is yours after you've paid the gear money. Who'd he get this from?

Ayla: This Kurdish boy. Arjîn, he says he knows you. And how would the girl charge a thousand? That's mad. After the malın parası *land money. Meaning the drugs become your property once you've paid this fee* has been paid there's going to be less than I wanted. You joking me.

Ali: That's why it's more sensible to work in McDonald's than this, but who's judging? It's a thousand because the water gets rocky in a split second, and the law. A quarter key puts you down for like five years. Where are you keeping it?

Ayla: In a suitcase. Enough questions now. If I had someone back on mainland I would do this all myself top to bottom. How much money do these men make and we see nothing of it?

The room goes quiet as Ayla picks up a pile of wadded-up tissue near the window and walks out of the room. She returns and her hands are wet from the sink. She wipes them on her trousers.

Ayla: Sorry, ant infestation. If I don't chuck this now I'm scared they're gonna lay eggs in my slipper.

Ali points a finger into her knee.

Ali: I know I put my money back into my country. When there's a vote I help out where I can. I'm a political man. We spend our money with our brains. If we all retired and took our kids to private school, where would we be?

Ayla: You don't take your kids to private school. Or any school.

Ali: Joke's on you, I don't have any. Your children are so perfect? Why does that one just hang around as if her head's going to start spinning like Şeytan.^{the Devil}

Turkish Cypriot

She looks to her side and Damla is trying to discreetly slip her hand down the sofa from behind them. A Nokia tune goes off.

Ali: One sec.

Ali walks into the hallway, looking ahead at the kitchen.

Makbule (from the back): Kim o? ^{Who's there?}

Turkish Cypriot

Ali (on his phone): Her mother speaks Turkish like she's been strangled. I'll ask her about it now, when does he want us to go? No chance we're getting Ufuk down there. Overbearing father? More like overbeating. All right, bye.

The phone gets slipped back into his pocket. Ali returns to the living room just as Damla walks out with İpek's armless doll, ready to return it. She gives him a dirty look until he is out of her line of sight.

Ayla: I wanted to ask you about the cabbages. Are you some kind of farmer?

He pushes a rollie towards her. Slender little thing.

AYLA AND HER CABBAGES: A BLUEPRINT OF A CONVERSATION

It is not daisy season in Kıbrıs. Nor are the acres of yellow-headed plants on Mesarya plain called oilseed rape. Instead, the fields are dotted with villagers who have come to collect lapsana now that its seeds are formed. Leave it much later than this and it will be animal feed, shovelled out to goats and cows. Crouching and picking at the wild mustard, everyone's outfits clothe the field in colours. Children sit eating leaves, watching their mothers yank at the ground. They walk back with armfuls of greens. Some carry wicker baskets dangling from forearms and stacked with greens.

One family fill old pillowcases with the plants. They come to a rest at a gnarled olive tree. Anne's back hurts from bending too much and she rubs it while she leans against the tree.

She complains to me about how they have nearly grown these vegetables out of existence – there have been too many generations of farmers trying to play with Allah and make cabbages out of mustard. Thank Him for Kıbrıs. She pulls out each leaf, smoothing them away from the coarse hairs of the stem. Under her fingers, the leaves seem due for snail fever, perforating at the roughness of her touch. In some places people call this a weed.

In our village and in our home, the garden had beef with the weeds. My mother grew her vegetables as though she hated lapsana. Everyone would come by the garden, 'Makbule abla! Makbule abla! Karpuzların baya büyüdü!' *Your melons have grown quite a bit!* My father avoided the garden. Allah rahmet eylesin. *God rest his soul* I don't remember ever seeing him grow for pleasure. Before the Cyprus war, he worked in the fields opposite the Mesarya plain but the house garden was Mum's project. And each plant was grown with a more scientific mind looking upon it.

Cabbage leaves, sun-crisped, were littered outside one morning. Cowboy tumbleweeds. The neighbour's dogs! The neat lines that Mum had dug and scraped straight, letting water travel stop by stop, were roughed up. I swept until my broom had a dead snail crunched into its straw. I thought: the leaves deserve more than a dead snail but the dead snail deserves to be shrouded in leaves. I swept and swept.

My mum woke up after me that day, and when she came to the garden, she crouched down by her cabbages and stroked each one, muttering. I looked at her skirt, its hem rubbing the ground. A shame to use your clothes as a broom; a basket, maybe, but not a broom. She didn't care to notice. For her, there was nothing to care about except hoping the cabbages would come back to life.

She said to me, 'Bahcende sihatlı bir yerdeyisen kafanda, her zaman hayat yapabilin.' *In your garden, if you're good in your head, you can always make life* She leant back on her heels and I saw the plants; they'd lost a few leaves but the inner heads were still there.

102

So yes, if you ask me about cabbages as a method of trans-
porting eroin, I know this. The Turkish variety are prized for
their enlarged leaf bud, that's where we put the heroin . . . You
let it grow around and you end up with perfect heroin sarma *stuffed leaves*
in tightly rolled cabbage leaves. Growing up in a garden, with
Anne who has her head in the mud, I can risk assess too. We
think about ways to maintain the structural integrity of the
lahana. I've picked cabbages from that garden and opening
up the leaves I've found dead bugs in the middle. You have
to look right into the centre of the thing, otherwise you're
going to eat something and not know about it.

If a bug can survive inside the cabbage, well you could
put the vegetables in the truck and carry those bugs a long
way. They'd go past the border, even as far as Germany. We
need to sell some actual cabbage in Germany to uphold the
business end of the business. Although the Germans naturally have their own cabbages, the Turkish product is popular
there. We should sell in January, when they're a seasonal
speciality. Everyone loves cabbage after Christmas. We can
position ourselves as a takeover company, and be the best
small importer in the West.

Imagine if one of our German customers was trying to
make themselves something nice and a bug spoilt the buy.
They'd chosen cabbage from this part of the world: they like
how thin our cabbage gets, it digests better. Each part of it is
loved, from zeytinyağlı lahana sarma *stuffed leaves in olive oil* to the turşu. *Turkish-style pickle*
But this pickle can be ruined. With fungus and weevils. One
time, my daughter's friend opened a bag of frozen spinach
and when the spinach started to sweat down in the pan, a
lump stayed too big . . . She looked and looked and looked,

do you know what she saw? It was a whole frog whose limbs started to unfurl as though it was going to come back to life. An entire Lazarus effect reserved for a frog. She hit that frog until it was flat on her spoon and then she tried to take a picture of the frog on the spoon to send to Tesco Customer Services. The Customer Services agent writes to her: 'From the picture provided it is unclear whether the frog you are suggesting you found in the product was actually found inside Tesco Value frozen spinach, or was indeed a frog.' Angela and her mum dealt with it properly, they took pictures and then sent half a frog body off in a ziplock bag to Tesco head-quarters. It didn't make the news the same way the KFC beak did a few years ago, but she did get some money for it. We don't have any money, so we should keep our (one or two) big customers happy.

The ancient Greeks said the cabbage plant pushed through the soil after Zeus's sweat fell onto the ground. A plant that's appropriately voracious in lifestyle. A child of a weed. It grows around whatever you put in the middle of it. Each plant equals one head, and if you sow twice annually there will be a supply all year long. This fact is wasted on me because I don't want to be involved in drugs. That's for the farmer and the chemist and Babo to deal with. I'm no farmer, just a gardener's daughter. So the inner heads of the cabbage need to be opened about twenty days into its life, and the rest of the time you grow it as our people have always done.

Kurmanji — *Ayla has enough respect for Babo to address him with this term. If Ayla was feeling forgetful, she might say 'Baba', the Turkish way. Although this would confuse him with her dad or a Turkish crime father, of which one is dead and the other irrelevant*

This is simply the beginning of another big rivalry, one that men are always going to be fighting. They mix together forever. In the Osmali times you would have the cabbage farmers of Merzifon calling themselves the Lahanacılar, to let everyone know 'The Cabbages' were coming. They treated cabbage as a deity presiding over sports matches and wars. Even the Merzifon cabbage team had their rivals: the Bamyacılar, the okra eaters. I dream of following the blueprint of the heroin shipment with smuggled lines of bullet-stuffed okra, its hairy skin a perfect body bag for their load.

I imagine everything you could do to transport heroin to London in a clever way. Where's the guarantee, by the way, that I get money for helping you? All I really want is for you to sell off the heroin that I have here, now that my baby daddy can't do it.

DAMLA, SAME DAY

I am in the garden and I think I see a rabbit. Something furry escaping through some chicken wire stacked at the end of the fence. I go to the wire and suddenly plastic comes towards me. A soup spoon swung straight at my face. It feels like getting hit in the nose with a roll of wrapping paper. I look up and my neighbour is looking down at me. He has been somewhere else for a long time, resting. He wears flip-flops even though it is winter, and I have never seen such big toes. His toes remind me of dates, full but greying in the cling film-wrapped packet. Crouching down, he pulls me through the hole in his fence and tells me I should never trespass. Behind him I see a black bag full of junk, old teddies and ladies' shoes. He sits on the grass in front of me and tells me to look under his dressing gown. Pretend it is a tent. Or a tepee is what them Indians call it. I'm too old for these games. I can make tea now and read now. My head is under the tent too fast and my face smushes against a lump of flesh. I keep my face scrunched up as though I'm in a bag of bugs on *I'm a Celeb*. He is still playing his music loud. It blasts from his house so all I can hear in the garden is Michael Jackson. He asks if my name is Damla like Dumb-la because I am so quiet and dumb dumb. I don't know how this is nothing, but it is. A few minutes of nothing. When I go back to my garden, İpek sees me crying and tells me to stop it, dumb dumb. I do. She throws her mud pie at my leg. I brush it off and stare at the woodlice that have been disturbed by her digging by a pile of old carpet in the front of the garden.

Nene is too unwell to defend me properly. She has propped the garden door open with a dining chair and sits there with her hands on her knees as if she is trying to push her feet down into the concrete patio. By her left foot is İpek's doll, whose legs are perfect shovels. She kicks it towards us.

—Eh, use this one, not your hands.

I turn towards her and my face is covered in mud. Hands too. Her face goes funny at me. I lean towards her and she goes more old-looking, all serious. She looks scared and doesn't hear me when I try to tell her that İpek started all this. İpek and the neighbour, but the neighbour is next door so we can tell İpek off instead.

—I'm sorry, kuzum, *my little lamb* you reminded your nene of someone. Stop going around looking like you've just been dug up out of the ground, go wash your face. It's like seeing a ghost!

When I go inside, I can't hear my mum speaking. I wash my face and the mud comes off it like it is mixed with sweat. The sink seems covered in milkshake now. I wipe the sink. Anne always tells me to wipe the sink after I use it, otherwise I might as well not bother. The sink is clean, the kettle is on and I am making tea. My nose hurts. I get the tray out.

BACK TO THE CHAT, SAME DAY

Damla walks in with a tray of biscuits and English tea. Her hands shake with the weight of the tray. She focuses carefully on the tea at the top so it doesn't leak. When she places it in front of the two of them, some spills and runs down the side onto the lace tablecloth that covers the stall in front of Ali and Ayla. Damla runs her index finger over her nose. She stands for a moment to see if her mum will react to the mark on her face and then slips out. They return to their conversation.

Ayla: It takes about twenty days, then you put the little bag in the middle and grow the leaves around it and off it comes to London. Just make sure nobody wants cabbage soup on the way.

Ali pulls a tissue out of his pocket and wipes the tray.

Ali: Anyway, I'm off now, minik Ayla. *Mini Ayla* No need to see me out.

As he stands he knocks the tray again, but this time all that slides loose is a biscuit. He grabs it as he walks towards the door.

Ayla: I went to go to my friend Sadi's house and he got a big brick through his window. Said a bunch of English boys did it. Know anything about that, Ali?

Leaning against the living room door, Ali throws two hands up and shrugs.

Ali: This country is going upside down, I tell you!

Ayla: Don't. He tells me he had this dumpy little Turkish man turn up at the shop a couple of weeks before this, asking for shop tax. Says the guy had a scar around his nose.

Ali: I ain't gonna lie. Before we worked together I saw this shop, beautiful income coming in but no one to look out for it, that's just how it goes. The world is not la la land.

Ayla: You don't make the rules for everything. Keep your hands off this. It won't be long till I've lost the shop anyway, I don't need you biting at my ankles while I'm on the floor.

Makbule, from outside: Why are you closing the door, be?

The door clicks back open. Slippers shuffle away.

Ayla: This is my character you're stamping. Sadi says he knows the look of a woman who likes trouble when he sees one. Has me labelled because of you. Do you know what it's like to lose just one person when you've built your people from the ground up?

Gold tooth laughter.

Ali: OK, I promise you I'll go right to Mehmet and whack him over the head with a stick, is that what you want to hear?

Ayla: Tamam Topuz Paşa, *OK, Prince of the Shepherd Staff* you do what's right.

Ali/Topuz Paşa: Bir elin nesi var, iki elin sesi var. *What does one hand have? Two hands make a sound.*

A PHEWW SOUND

Today Moruk Cafe is not busy. It is raining so much that the day is dogged by the sound of people smacking their feet on the way in. Agata has come by to open up, but she's sat at the TV watching footage of an earthquake in İzmit. The camera zooms in on a dismembered Barbie doll, trapped under concrete that's soft as dust. Three men are not bothered by the news story. They are leaning close to each other on a table that has a red velvet tablecloth over it. Mehmet has just given up doodling; his pen keeps going through the paper.

Ali: Heard about Sadi, you thought you'd scare him into wanting a safety blanket and instead you suffocated him with it.

Ufuk: What should we do? Get the kids to write him a letter of apology for the damage they caused to his window?

Mehmet: Should we get in touch and offer to pay?

A pheww sound comes whistling through Topuz Paşa's teeth.

Ali: I'm not getting mixed up with this victim stuff. If they want to get back the money they can take a bunch of children to court or wait for their insurance to pay up.

Mehmet (bombastically): This was all pointless anyway because now Ali has himself fancying the owner's woman.

Ali: It's not about that, I've just got my brain on. Now she's got nobody to run the shop for her and she can't afford to keep it running, that money is going to run out fast.

Mehmet: Why are you thinking about this? Get her baby daddy to deal with it, he's probably rolling on his back laughing how you're sweeping up his shit.

Ali puts his hands over his face. His index finger presses in on the bridge of his nose.

Ali: It sounds like the shop is headed to close with no one to run it or not. Just drop it, yeah?

Ufuk: Have you spoken to them about the cabbage?

Mehmet: Yes, me and Ali tried to get you on the phone but you were too busy harassing your daughter.

Ufuk: Don't get involved, man. Who are you? If you had a daughter she'd be a car wash.

Mehmet: Doesn't sound far from what I've heard about Filiz. Someone says they saw Arj giving her a freebie.

The room is quiet as Ufuk processes Mehmet's words, and remains so as he takes his things and walks out.

MAKBULE HAS FRIENDS,
OCTOBER 1999

Panny has come over to moan. He normally shouts 'yaho' when he arrives at the house. He comes from the garden entrance, which is padlocked usually. Having access from the back of the house is the bane of Ayla's life, it leads up to the garden from the main street, and attracts boys who use the loose bricks along the ginnel to build a platform to stand on and poke their heads over the fence. Those boys are the nice ones because the fence has been repaired on multiple occasions when someone has kicked at the wood to see what's behind it. Panny has left his wife Andrea at home while he comes to see Ayla. Aside from the fact that she is not physically present by his side, he walks with more gaiety in his step when she's not there. As he approaches the garden door, spit comes flying towards his foot.

Panny: What the fucking hell, man, you jokin me? Ayla, where are you be?

The neighbour's fence rattles as he pushes the slats back into place.

Turkish Cypriot Ayla (from the kitchen): Ooooo, Panny Bey, *Mr Panny* come in, come in. My mum's going to be happy to see you. I've propped her up with some cushions in the front room.

Panny: You need to sort out your bloody creep neighbour. If he harasses me one more time I'm going to call the police on him.

Ayla leans over from the sink where she's washing up to kiss Panny hello on his cheeks. He sits down to watch her, putting his shopping bags by his feet.

Ayla: Oh, what's he done now? I avoid him so much, you know? The kids hate him, especially Damla. I think it's because he stares a lot, you know, but he's not well. I tell him not to look at us and he stops but then he still gives us a funny feeling.

Panny: Make sure they're never in the garden alone. Men like that test where they can start and stop, Ayla.

İpek comes into the kitchen. She looks older than six but this could be because of her height. She has not taken after her mum here.

Panny: Manamou, İpek's getting big, isn't she?

Ayla: She is. I can't keep up with them.

Panny: Eh, how's Makbule doing?

Ayla: Oh, she'll be happy to see you, in the front room. If you're going that way bring her some helim karpuzi. *watermelon with helim cheese* Turkish Cypriot

Panny puts his bags in a cupboard before taking the tray. It is heavy. When he gets to the front room, Makbule's feet are poking out from the blanket that she's swaddled in.

Panny: Ti egine? *What's up?* Greek

Makbule: Offf be, I'm fine. Tell my daughter not to fuss with all the food. I'm going to have a nap.

She turns her head to the ceiling and pantomimes being fast asleep. Panny doesn't laugh.

Panny: Ayla was telling me on the phone that you got scared in front of Damla. Are you thinking of him again?

Panny sits on the couch and squeezes Makbule's hand.

Makbule: It was nothing, Panny Bey, I just wasn't expecting her to come out the garden one day with mud all over her face and it gave me a bit of a shock. I'm so old these days that a shock gives me the flu, I tell you.

Panny stands up to go, taking the tray with him.

Panny: Try not to see a lion in a kitten, these things grow the more you think about them.

The door closes. In the kitchen, Ayla is eating karpuz, _watermelon_ which she nearly spits out when she sees that she is eating and her guest is not.

Ayla: Is that it? I thought you was going to eat some with Mum or I would have waited.

Panny: No, no, no. Andrea put me some at home. I'm stressed, man. Some boys living in my house downstairs are killing me.

Ayla: How?

A plate of fruit and cheese gets put down in front of Panny. He picks up a dessert fork from it and starts eating without even realising it.

Panny: They spend all their days inside a cafe on Factory Road, then when they get home all I can smell is that shit coming out from under their door.

Ayla: Language.

Panny whacks his thigh in shame and frustration.

Panny: Ah, sorry, Ayla-mou. So I go to their door and tuck tuck on it to ask for my rent. It's been one month now and they're not opening the door!

Ayla: You have to nip it in the bud now.

Damla has walked in. She checks out the garden door. It is raining outside. İpek follows her.

114

Panny: Tenants like this . . . you have to cut the electricity and everything to get them out the house, it shouldn't have to come to this. Just pay your bill, man! But you know what? They did!

The girls giggle and imitate him.

—Just pay your bill, man!

Ayla: Girls, go put your bums on chairs. There's karpuz on the table. That's interesting, Panny, they paid?

Panny: Where's Erhan? Yes, they did! They said a Turkish friend of mine spoke to them. I have a mystery mate somewhere.

Ayla: My friend Zade just came to take him. She has a son his age, Warren.

Panny: Be, why didn't you get her to take the rest?

Ayla: One is enough to make my life easier, trust me. But that's nice with your rent at least, until you get them out.

Panny: Yes, yes. Anyway, let me go, if I eat too much here Andrea will deliberately make something extra nice that I'm too full to eat.

Ayla: To prove you a lesson, yeah? Good one. Take care, Panny Bey.

SNOOKER HALL, OCTOBER 1999

There is a strong cigarette smell passing through the club. Weed intertwining with it in a tag-along way. If you have a skilful nose you may be able to catch the kebab shop underneath too. The logo by the entrance and leading up the stairs into the place is the neon outline of a man who is bent over a table with a snooker cue burrowing into it. His backside pops cheekily up, as though the sign belongs in Soho. Underneath the clattering of snooker balls there is a steady thrum of conversation. The bar is cash only. People can get a coffee here and it will be crema froth perfection, but if they can afford the drinks, they'll probably lime up their lips when they smell soggy cardboard on the beer. You can pay for a set of games and get some drinks thrown in on top of that, which is probably the best deal if you want value for money. It's a busy mess. At the back of the room there's a TV on a wall mount. When that first went up, some customers complained about it damaging the wood-panelled walls. If you go up one more floor you'll find more tables with bigger pockets, but that area is usually closed off. You can play till the early morning, and there are a few groups here who have come for a four-hour session. Some didn't pay anything for entry. Management says it's because they're regulars, but they're regulars because they don't pay anything for entry. It's not your standard place, though. They have a pool shop selling Peradon cues and clients who like to turn those into splinter hazards.

At Table 4, a stout man in a jacket too warm for the inside is setting the table for a game. He forgets how to every time, so whispers the mnemonic 'God Bless You' to lay out the colours: green, brown, yellow, and then the rest.

Rohan: Andrej, bet you a hundred I'll win.

Andrej: Immigration are looking for you, mate, you should be worried about that.

Rohan: Shut up, jobcentre are looking for you for this year's tax returns.

He strikes the white. The object ball goes straight to the middle pocket.

Andrej: How do you do this, middle pocket is my worst enemy. How're you finding the job anyway, Rohan?

Rohan: It's all right, I've got my grillside routine perfecto. Crazy customers . . . they can't understand when you explain them that one cheese no cheese is a ham . . . What we can do?

He plays the cue ball, trying to segment the shot, but misses entirely. He swears.

Andrej: I know, crazy tills, innit. When it's like that I have to have two cappuccinos with seven sugars each.

Rohan: You should see my face when I get ten grill slips in five minutes.

Andrej (conspiratorially): That's your time to go off and do a ten-minute sweep and mop. I'm going to actually teach you how to take the temperature of the burgers.

Rohan: Thinking you're the new manager all of a sudden?

Rohan laughs and tries to pot the ball. He misses again.

Rohan: Sweep and mop manager more like.

Andrej: Just cause all you're doing is packing Big Macs.

Rohan: I would be, but it's a reduced schedule, innit.

Behind them, a man with a cola-bottle body walks over to Table 5. It instantly clears at his approach.

Andrej: That's because they're wasting the rota on old Osias.

Rohan: Yeah, the man's too lazy.

Andrej: You should let him work, man, put him on grillside and take a smoke break.

A man runs over with a chair and puts it down at Table 5. Cola Man sits down. Their conversation continues.

Rohan: No, I'm the grill man. One Big Mac, one quarter, three cheese, two double, one ham. Busy no busy, follow-the-chart-fresh-food, innit.

Andrej: I just wrote timers in my language. Cheese, syr: expected time, then pickles.

Rohan: Jeden hamburguer iba syr. One hamburger. I'm learning.

Andrej: Well done, but hamburger is bez syr-a in Slovak.

Someone runs into the room. He has leaflets in his hand.

Leaflet Man: You can live forever, but not by the agenda. We were designed with a treasure, an Immortal Soul-Joy nature! Don't take the chip and let AI control you.

He leaves but not before dashing a stack of leaflets onto Table 4. All of the balls scatter as Rohan and Andrej protest. Ufuk has just walked into the snooker club and he looks pumped. Like anger or like extreme enthusiasm for a football match. He approaches Babo, who is at Table 5, and puts his keys down on the table. They make a try at some greetings before Ufuk gets to the point.

Ufuk: Abi, you need to tell your boy Arj to stop speaking to my daughter.

Babo: Kardaş, you have it wrong. He's not speaking to Filiz, he's selling to her. Better than that guy from the pound shop always buying her gold when he had a wife.

Ufuk: Is this what you want me to believe? With what money, eh? She comes home with the same amount that she left with.

Babo touches his chin in a gesture of disappointment, like a wizard pulling out his beard in front of him.

Babo: Hold yourself, Ufuk. That's because I gave it free when I saw whose daughter it was. She likes to talk about her dad when she comes. Selling fruit on Lordship Lane?

Ufuk grits his teeth. He nods, apologises, then picks up his keys off the side of the snooker table before walking out. Rohan patiently resets his table.

CALEDONIAN ROAD,
SAME DAY

A sign sectioning off legal visits and social visits is the first piece of signage you see when you approach the prison visitors' centre. After this, a parking sign. It refers to this building as an establishment and it is indeed an establishment in the sense that it seems to be part of a wider construct, housing many who are anti-establishment. It is a system organised by law. But that's where the term falls loose, because today it is out of kilter with similar centres in the area. There has been a parking disaster. Neither the Crown nor any servant or agents of the Crown are to be held liable for any losses or damages to the cars in the lot. This is particularly frustrating for those who have driven to visit their loved ones today and have left their cars at their own risk. When leaving a car at their own risk, drivers don't imagine a distressed pensioner smashing every windscreen with a plastic bag full of tinned goods. The tins don't do much damage but she is persistent until she is stopped. As Ayla approaches the visitors' centre with her three children, she admires the woman's tenacity and spirit. Ayla has taken the bus with the kids today and for the first time this feels like the superior option. Generally, security is decent around this part but law enforcement is slow when the vehicular assailant that they have to immobilise is a small Irish woman with a loose wig and a weaponised Kwik Save bag.

Ayla thinks to herself that she is safe because it is a woman and not a man, and walks ahead to the entrance of the centre. Upon arrival, she signs in and gives in her pass from her previous visit to get through to the waiting area. The kids ask for sweets from the canteen and books from the play area. To the officers in the window booth, she gives magazines, £30 and tracksuit bottoms. Inside, everyone is fighting to the front of the queue to get their visitor pass before they run out. There are never enough passes. The kids in the room watch their families get jostled.

When they are called in, they look for where he is. One of many men seated at a table and waiting for his family – Ayla is surprised again to see him without his curls. He has gone for a close crop, so his children are disappointed by him before he has even hugged them or spoken to them. They accuse him of doing this big shave without their prior knowledge and it is as though he has broken a pact with them, especially İpek, who cares about her dad's hair very much. Until this moment, she had been using it to remember him by and now she will have to focus on his nose or some other thing that hadn't struck her quite the same way. He still smells like Old Holborn. İpek tries to sit on his lap, he tells her that she needs to sit as if she is riding a horse sideways, like a lady. Without his hair combed through with oil, there is less oomph to him than Ayla is used to. She is happy to see he's gained weight but sad to see that prison food has done most of the hard work here.

—Erhan, come closer, you know you have big hands, little king, who'd you get that from, do you think?

He holds his hands up to his son's. They swamp them but to Erhan, for a brief moment as he moves his hands forward, they look the same size. İpek tries to push her hand in between so she can join in. Damla notices a gesture from her mum and takes the two over to a bead maze in the corner, where they push blocks along a looping path.

—How's your mum?

Ayla gestures towards the children. It is like she has lost her voice.

—I'm worried the kids are going to make her more scared. She keeps having nightmares but they frighten her too sometimes.

—Send her good health from me, if she'll accept it.

—Probably not.

She makes him laugh and misses him more because of this. It is almost easier when he is angry, and therefore less the man she misses.

—Anyway, I'm going to send my friends to you. When they come they'll take what I've got back at yours and they'll make everything clean again, OK?

—This is what I wanted to talk to you about.

—OK, go on.

They try to speak in code.

—You remember Ali? We spoke, he came to me and he offered to help shift the shopping for us, so I said yes. Yes please!

—Why are you letting him touch my shopping for?

—The plan is to share your shopping through different routes, then he takes a cut of the profits and everyone is happy.

Leaning forward to whisper more, Ayla drops her volume.

—He's even got me in touch with that Kurdish boy Arj, who tells me their Babo is very interested in my ideas. The cabbage one too!

—It's like you're not even thinking of the kids' future. Why would you even risk doing something yourself? So how does this work out step by step? What are you seeing?

—I help Ali with some cabbage plans and he helps me shift the shopping, simple. This is me thinking 'future future'.

He holds her hand across the table like a nurse placating a patient.

—Running a vegetable shop on Lordship Lane and dealing with vegetables are different. There's two things I fear right now: I fear God and I fear you with your plans. I can't get to you. You're not communicating with me.

—I've just been trying to do what's best, there's no training for this. I can't send you a letter by budgie. What can I say? You did this.

On her way out – with the kids at her sides – Ayla gets stopped and checked again. She is told they need to do a pat-down but refuses until the female officer returns from the toilet. When the officer comes out of the toilet, her hands are still slightly damp when she gloves up. The gloves are thick enough to protect her from anything sharp in someone's clothes but Ayla still imagines the bathroom water seeping through.

DAMLA, THE DAY AFTER DAMLA'S DAD GOT ARRESTED, 1998

This is one of the first Sundays when Erhan isn't crying. I've resented him since he was born. Anne is more anxious now around my dad. She gets more edgy with me if I am too . . . myself. I am six and he tells me that I'm the only child of his who isn't an Irish twin. That İpek and Erhan practically knew each other in the womb. Erhan is two and İpek is three. What is an Irish twin? He tells me it is when a mum and a dad are in a competition with the rest of the world to have kids the fastest. They've won now (because of İpek and Erhan), so they can stop for a bit.

I think maybe that Anne would probably have liked to stop with me. We had a routine before my brother and my sister. She did gym stretches with me so she could be the strongest fittest mum she could be. She always tried to get me to touch my toes. On her bed, I would lean forwards to touch my toes until I fell to my side. Now she always asks me to watch them and be a big girl. Zade never asks me to be a big girl. She has a two-year-old too. She doesn't let me near him, says I'm too young and I might squash the boy's head.

Today Erhan is not crying but Anne is. She is putting wet

clothes out to dry. I recognise them as big man clothes. Ironing too, these shirts, and she is ironing all the way to the bottom of some jeans so they are boxed at the edges. Nene is telling her not to bother ironing because nobody is going to care about the creases after they've been left in the cupboard for a few years.

A few years.

Nene's feet smell but I still sit by them because she is warm. They do not smell bad like big dolma *stuffed vine leaves* but bad like medicine. She used to enjoy crochet work. The cupboards in the kitchen are draped with her lacework, as well as her chair. The chair smells of pee, she does it without noticing, little by little. She calls over to Anne from her armchair, cracks jokes to put the tears away.

—If you cry too much you'll drown us in the lake!

If my mum drowned me, she would be so sad she'd cry even more. If there was a chance that I might not have drowned, I definitely would then. Anne comes over to us, pairing his socks.

—Where's the suit socks?

What's a suit sock? The ones that are meant to show from the shoe. Softest of the odds. Anne won't tell me what he did to go to jail. The more I ask the less she keeps her normal voice and gets her witch one instead. The socks are getting pulled long before getting tucked in together, angry pulls as if she is trying to kill the socks. Nene tells her to calm down. Stop cleaning.

I never really called him Baba. Said Dracula to him instead. He had such pointy teeth and let me touch them till my finger would go yellow and start to feel like a bite. These are things to miss now. You can miss things you never really knew, like İpek and Erhan, or miss them like me.

AYLA,
NEW YEAR'S EVE, 1999

We went to Tesco and bought a New Year kit with hats – silver bowler hats. The packed aisles were nearly emptied by rushing ravers, whistle packs in hand, the fiercely intricate bargain signs drawing them all in the same direction. On a far corner of the toiletry shelves someone had left behind a swathe of NYE odds and ends, enough for us to grab and go. Parties, Zade says, are getting too expensive to be fun. We are staying in tonight, with the kids. She's bringing her little one, who loves Erhan and İpek (Damla too if she can come out of her head).

Their dad is not here.

Parties suited us so much; if you have me dancing then you have me. I remember the symmetry that we had in that way when we met, and I knew that in some roundabout way, whether sober or in a dream, he had met me before. It's hard to dance now, to keep dancing when it feels like I'm signalling him. At the counters, we both apologise to the lady at the till because she is working and we are not. British guilt, apologising for spending money just like the people who apologise to us at work.

Getting home we are accosted by a woman outside Zade's house who is determined to air her dirty laundry to the whole street. In a street where people do that kind of airing on a daily basis, our reactions are quiet and unembarrassed. Both neighbour and friend, Zade knows I am only ever twenty seconds away and is constantly aware of me struggling in those smaller private ways, trying to get the shopping in or avoid men at my back. A look tells me to turn away. She needs her privacy now.

Zade is so stingy she drops you like a bag of flour when you ask for anything, according to her sister. Actually, Zade is now careful with her son around idle men because of her sister's boyfriend. The money she asks Zade for feeds Topuz Paşa's chain, there's no ignoring this.

The millennium is a family thing. We will have the TV on with the rest of the country. Big Ben. The man next door comes to the door with presents for the kids, baby dolls for them all even though Damla is eight. She looks at the doll as if she is about to poke its eyes out.

We put foil streamers from wall to wall in the front room while Zade tells me what it's been like for her on her latest cleaning job. A corporate booking. They were rude to her last week, so this week she has started shredding documents at random. Page 52 out of a 100-page stack, and so on. I feel the same frustration at the Post Office, and count my other options. People like Arjîn come by to pocket unemployment, only to go and get cash in hand from Babo. This year I am starting it almost exactly the way he is.

DEBATES AT MORUK,
1 JANUARY 2000

On the TV, the news channel cuts to an American man handing out his award for 'the person of the Full Millennium' posthumously to Mustafa Kemal Atatürk. The host is happy about the abolishment of the Ottoman sultanate, and tells his audience that Atatürk was the only leader in history to successfully turn a Muslim nation into a Western parliamentary democracy and secular state. The anchorwoman on Kanal D returns to front camera with a smile, before signing off for the morning. Upon her digital departure, a collective groan springs up amongst the enamoured men in Moruk cafe. One man slaps the TV and gets up to go to the toilet. Mehmet playfully pushes the plastic chair that Ali is sitting in, making it wobble under pressure. They begin:

Mehmet: Forget Atatürk, what you call Atatürkism I call a con. My father was one of the smartest men going and then suddenly one of the thickest, course he was pissed off.

Ali: Explain how it's a con to make an entire language for your people. You try do that yourself and all you'll come out with is eşek *donkey* hoo-ha noises. You expect us to stay on the coat-tails of the Arabs.

Mehmet: Who put this fear of Arabs in you but Atatürk?

Mehmet: You're quiet because I've got you! Bir gün akşam olur bizde gideriz, kalır dudaklarda şarkımız bizim. We've lost our past to keep up with one man's future. *One day we will go too, and all we'll have on our lips are our song. Necip Fazıl quote*

Ali: Quoting from Necip Fazıl, the great fan of ethnic cleansing? Shut up, man, shut up, Yusuf abi's coming in and the last thing I need is you putting him in a bad mood.

Mehmet: Ulan! *Derogatory, like 'son of a'*

Mehmet leans forward to chuck his water at Ali's feet. Usually the gesture is a blessing, water is cast for a journey to come and go as easily as water does.

Mehmet: Without your language you own nothing; everything is just toilet paper if you can't read it, Ali Bey. Nothing in Topkapı library makes sense to us any more. Who have we got to blame for that?

Ali: You've got too much time on your hands. Selam, Yusuf abi. *elder brother*

Yusuf: Selam, abim.

Mehmet jostles past Ali to get up and kiss Yusuf's hand, but is turned away, getting a soft backhand instead. The fleece Yusuf wears smells of cooked yet unseasoned okra.

Yusuf: Herkes aklını pazara çıkarmış, yine kendi aklını beğenmiş. *They put up minds for sale on the market, everyone liked his own mind*

Mehmet: Ufuk told me to tell you he won't be coming to talk with you today, massive time waste but it's his daughter again. She's big trouble, you know – seeing that Arj boy. It would be so funny if I didn't know what Ufuk was like.

This news comes like fresh air to Yusuf. He was going to miss out on his daughter's birthday to talk business, but, for now, he can do what he wants to do. Not without taking a mental note of Ufuk's disrespect.

YUSUF ABI'S
LOVELY FACTORY

The first time the police came for me, they came into my house and smelt weed. The way they barged past my mother (who was alive then) made me so angry... I could have been arrested there and then. Off they went straight into the kitchen and that's where they found my wife cooking molohiya. *Turkish Cypriot stew made from a weed-smelling weed. From the Arabic 'molokia': for royalty* She offered them some so sweetly, that woman is always so sweet. After lifting up the lid, they looked at my wife and couldn't stop laughing before they apologised and left. This is back when the police had curly sideburns.

I go way back. Coming from Kıbrıs, the first need of mine was a house, and the nicest man took me in, a mainlander called Muharrem. He had a beautiful wife too and her cooking was unbeatable, much to my wife's annoyance in the years to come. He was a very good fellow and he gave me a job. Made me a factory man and gave me a couple of hundred skirts. The first payment I remember . . . I gave him the goods, he counted the money while he was sitting, one leg on the other. I thought he was going to give it to me and I opened my hand for the money but he threw it to the floor. Can you imagine how upset I was? He said to me that you pick up your money from the floor if it is your first money.

Muharrem used to pay £25 a week, a small room – his first factory was one room.

One buttonhole machine, one hole press. He was by himself and then his wife came home from dropping the kids to school and she helped him as well, picking up a hundred, two hundred, sometimes five hundred a week. Then he moved to a bigger place, he set himself a goal of making fifteen hundred to two thousand a week, then I helped and brought some friends to come in as machinists. We got so many workers around us. One day his brothers came to him and told him to upsize, they found a two-floor place for us all to move to. It was a lovely factory; everywhere there's windows, central heating, two lifts and parking spaces. Muharrem said OK and we moved there, and there he made his money, so I made my money. Whatever I worked for, he looked after me and gave me plenty work, much as I want. Honest man. When I delivered my work, everything was cleanly given, bundle by bundle, all the cotton has been cut and there's no excess on it. I knew what I was doing from home.

We ended up teaming together properly in the factory, too. I'm a worker who has workers now. Always listening to people, always polite with people. If people do good work that week, I give extra money in their envelope (sometimes £30 extra).

Muharrem didn't know I was doing dodgy work. One day my wife went up to him and asked him to talk me out of the betting office. The man took me to the betting office and it worked as they hoped, I couldn't gamble in front of a straight man. But my wife got in my business again, she told Muharrem not to let me bring a particular friend of mine onto the factory floor. That's exactly what he did and so the next day he came to me and said it was a factory – a business, not a playground. We still saw each other outside though, my friend and me.

Muharrem went to jail for a few months for me, which I do remember (he finds it hard to let me forget). I don't mix with him so much now. It became like vegetable soup, everyone grassing everyone up.

It went like this: we were going for a meeting, Muharrem and I. I suggested he met me at the location but if he wouldn't mind just keeping a box of clothes in his boot . . . Soon as he come out from the factory, he looked in his mirrors and noticed someone following him. A Ford Capri. Green colour. Another car come, same model but black. Driving by Madame Tussauds, he looked out to see he has a taxi on his right side but it's going exactly the same speed. The driver is almost winking at Muharrem, trying to show him his customer. This passenger, smart guy with tie, had a newspaper in his hand but was looking at him from the side of his eye before the taxi driver rolled down his window.

He started to slow but he looked to his left and there I was, these men already stopped me. In his 2.8 Granada, big solid car, he cut through the police roadblock and sent all the cars spinning. Even a policewoman jumping in the road didn't stop him, he tapped her out the way (she was fine). He drove until he got to a shopping city with enough people to feel safe, and parked up to wait. Plain clothes got him! In questioning, all he told them was to hurry up because he had a meeting later, that's how sure he was that they had nothing on him. That's when they promised him he wouldn't see Christmas.

Now he understood why I didn't come with him in his car and he started to look at that box of samples differently. They got him for cannabis, intention to supply a Class B drug. This is why you have to cover your own back, make the little moves that protect you from things going wrong. As I said, Muharrem still doesn't let me forget it.

The way I work with business? Say the man across the road does only one thing better than me and it's lahmacun; *Turkish pizza* the first thing I'll do is start to stock lahmacun. It will be a priority to get the fluffiest base, the most parsley. Whatever it takes. You see what I mean?

TOPUZ PAŞA VISITS
AYLA AGAIN, 2000

On Ayla's legs, Erhan is sleeping. Just past the terrible twos, he now sleeps easier. He has always enjoyed being rocked by her, works a charm for each of Ayla's children. Beneath the pillow, her legs have gone blotchy from the weight of the child. The doorbell goes and she hears her mum sigh from the kitchen. Ayla needs to answer the door first. She wakes her son, trying to ease the pillow to her left, his head slips off the pillow and the crying starts up. Crying son at the hip, the front door is opened to Topuz Paşa.

Topuz Paşa is at the door in a black leather waistcoat, granddad shirt underneath. Leather smells activated by his sweat. Damla comes to take Erhan's hand and bring him into the kitchen, where her nene is sitting in the lace armchair. İpek is nowhere to be seen.

A man with a mission, there are no hellos to Damla or Erhan, just a watch-tapping triteness. Perhaps another man would have wanted to prove kindness, gesture towards crying baby and make chat. Babo has been on the phone and when Babo gets on the phone, people don't give him a reason to ring again. Topuz Paşa is to talk about cabbages today. Ayla takes him through to the sitting room and calls Damla for biscuits and tea.

Ayla: Is everything good now? Can we get rid of my stuff, I don't want it sitting around the house too long... especially if that Babo knows it's here.

Topuz Paşa: Yes, but first I wanted to talk about the cabbages.

Ayla: Yes, I'll talk about it soon. Tea first?

Topuz Paşa: If I think about it, this conversation is no big deal really, to let you sell what your baby daddy couldn't.

Ayla: You're letting me? We know you're not big boss, don't try it.

Topuz Paşa: You got me. Where's your kids?

Making a show of looking around, left, right and left again, Topuz Paşa elicits a laugh from Ayla.

Ayla: Damla's just there with the tea.

Topuz Paşa: Shake any more and you'll drop the tray, kız! [girl]

Ayla: Leave her, she'll get better with practice.

Damla doesn't spill any tea as she sets the tea down. Her nan waits in her armchair for her to come back and put the biscuit tin away. When she lingers around adults too long, she gets snapped at, so she goes quickly, the frame on the living room door rattling at her departure.

Topuz Paşa: Ufuk's daughter is Damla's age. You should let them play together.

Ayla: The curly-haired girl? I've seen her riding her bike around the estate...

Topuz Paşa: He's strict on his girls, has to be cos his older one, Filiz, is a bit of a stress.

Ayla: I like the sound of her already.

Topuz Paşa: Have you had a chance to think about how to package the cabbage?

Makbule walks in, slow on her legs. Having left Erhan and İpek with their sister, she tries to stretch out her time away from them. Leaning on the wall, she looks to Topuz Paşa.

Makbule: You're doing şeytan work with my daughter, aren't you?

Topuz Paşa: Nothing like that, abla, I'm just helping your daughter. *[sister]*

Ayla puts her hands up to warn her mum.

Ayla: Anne, please, uzatma. *[don't long this out]*

Makbule (while running over her chin hair): So what does it smell like then, Ali Bey? *[Mr Ali]* This stuff I see under our kitchen sink. Nearly flushed it down the toilet.

Topuz Paşa: Poison.

Makbule: Tabiki, *[of course]* but what does this 'poison' smell like?

Topuz Paşa looks to Ayla for permission before continuing.

Topuz Paşa: Bitter?

Makbule: What's the problem with bitta? *[Turkish Cypriot olive bread]*

Turkish Cypriot Ayla: No be, bi-tterrr. Olive bread mış. *[Onomatopoeic, represents the feeling of 'as if']*

Makbule: Snap at me again and I'll put you in the potato pot to boil.

With her chest pumped up, outrage or pride, Makbule leaves the room, but not before wedging the door open with a plastic slipper. The slipper makes a squelching sound as it is shoved under the gap.

Ayla: Sorry, where did I leave off?

AYLA CONTINUES TALKING,
SAME DAY

Black opium comes past the border ready for one of yours to mix it with chemical from the red-top bottles. Your chemist turns it into the dust, however he does that.

Imagine you're in a room. An entire wall is covered in eroin, separated into anahtar. _key, for kilo_ Each key stacked up to the ceiling. Someone has come along with a big felt blanket and tucked it in. You can't see it but you feel the energy of it in the room. These dealers charge more since the millennium; depending on how the streets are, you can sell one anahtar for up to twenty-five thousand. If you're a supplier fresh off a plane who has just spent six hours flying to Istanbul and another hour in a car, your nerves stand on end. You feel fear in your mouth. Clenched teeth, straight through the gum up into your ears and burning with fear.

This is why the staging area sets a precedent for everything. Fresh from the Golden Crescent, it is the most creative yet disciplined point of the entire journey. There are no half-measures when it comes to this cabbage implantation period. You have to grow the cabbages in with onions set around them, so no flies settle, and again I would remind you about keeping their structural integrity.

In all businesses, you need a 'fall guy case study'. It is always good to look at those who have failed before you. The Ukrainians had a bit of a cabbage operation going . . .

They didn't have it going in the same way. The Ukrainians' plan was to bring drugs into a prison using a wheelie cart filled with hollowed-out cabbages. One of the screws just so happened to rest his hand on one and in it went, finding a bowl of rotten leaf and some cigarette packets. This is why my thinking changed: I wanted to demonstrate to you that I have a good set of core skills. Risk assessment. I am good at evaluating previous 'projects' and can set out how we can avoid this type of failure occurring again. I want to tighten the logistical side of things, and focus on how we prepare. You must circumvent the suspicion that a cabbage is not solid the whole way through. This is the responsibility you're speaking about, where you are the one to do things right to the end of the tape measure. Recognising the botanical potential that can come from a transportation method like this is crucial – this is a full-on operation, not just a cabbage head hollowed out with items inside. Instead, find yourself with a weight-consistent truckload of home-grown cabbages with a baggie of eroin inside that isn't heavy enough to set things off. It takes about twenty days for the bud to grow and open up, then you put the little eroin bag in the middle and wait to grow the leaves around it and off it comes to London. Just make sure nobody fancies lahana çorbacık ^{lil cabbage soup} on the way. ^Turkish Cypriot^

When the farmer has met with your chemist and your chemist has got his dust ready for your little workers to sort this into cabbage, a branded lorry will set off from Midyat. I think you should have something like 'Mardin Din Din' printed onto it.

DAMLA: MEETING CEMILE, 2000

When Anne comes in she tells me I have a visitor. A new friend for a new century. I ask her what's the word for century when it's in the thousands and she doesn't know. Bin-something.

I meet her, hair first. She stands at arm's length from her dad, Ufuk, and her mum, who doesn't give her name to me. It's rude that the girl laughs at me. Apparently I stare, and Ufuk whispers about creepy kids who stare.

—Tell her if she looks like that for too long and the wind changes she'll get stuck with that şeytan face. Go on, talk to her, Cemile.

Cemile. Like the girl in my class, Jamilah. Jamilah for kind, beautiful. I don't know if Cemile is kind. What a nice name. Reminds me of the window. Our garden has cemile, too. We often collect the fallen petals: İpek, Erhan and I. When we have gathered the petals, we put them in a glass of water until we put so many that the petals sink to the bottom and go brown. I always wanted to see what they looked like after they went brown but Nene throws them away by then.

Cemile has turned up in a sheepskin coat and when she bends over to pick up one of my drawings, she looks like the Simpsons' dog with stilts for legs. We look at each other, knowing about our two-way looking. Those drawings were supposed to be hidden away by now, drawings of tents and rabbits getting lost. We keep looking at each other looking; our longest look eventually broken by her eyeing my tents and rabbits. My eyes pass hers to look at the bike behind her. Her dad has brought it in and I can tell Anne is annoyed that an outside thing has come inside.

Nobody ever taught me to cycle. It's never too late, no, but I don't want to learn. Nene says it is expensive buying a bike, what for when the English government give you buses; sometimes you can even go with trains. If you want to go to the park, you can run to the park. If you don't want to run, then you can walk through the alley that takes you down to Lordship Rec, if you walk even more you can go all the way through the grass to the bit where the Moselle needs to be pumped through so that it gets the right kind of water in, instead of the wrong kind of water. Brown. Murky. Some shoes floating. All different types of shoes, brown leather ones and Velcro black and whites. Floating on the water, chucked there by someone who isn't grateful for what they have. I still want to take the bike, though, so when Cemile offers to ride with me perched on the back, I'm gone as soon as Anne lets me.

Us kids in twos   biking like whistles
going
    between
bits
        of wind.
            My fingers pinching in her belly.

Go a bit slower when there's people in the way!
Cemile?   Cemile!
Dirty pavement cracking at the wheels.
Bits more wind and bits more wobble.

Pavement starts to blend into grass. She's leading us
with a map in her head, past a small hedge that looks
forest-ready   through Lordship Rec.
dodging benches in bushes like old cars,
towards Farm.

Moselle water sounds in my head.
If you listen close, the water sounds friendly as steel
pans around here.

Then we're turning down a path that goes towards a line of
bollards – the kind of posts you can leap over easily. Off
the bike quickly. A one-handed spring leap, legs out daddy-
long-legs girl. Back on the bike. I get my courage here and
hold my hands out to the left and right for more than a split
second, legs pinning on her hips. When I scrape my nail on
one bollard, I pull my arms quick back in and hold Cemile
again. She finally swings our bike to a stop by an upside-down
couch that looks like it's been thrown off the roof of a car.

The black sheeny material under the couch has little pools
of rainwater collecting in its lumps and bumps. There's a
tear in the corner and inside this I see a little ziplock bag
winking at me. I want to put my hand in but I'm scared that
there'll be a rat there waiting to get craned out of the corner
clinging on one of my fingers. I think this a lot when I see

people playing at a claw crane, fishing around in a bunch of soft toys, never sure what hell they're gonna pull out. I don't want the bag with the stuff in enough to risk a rat. Besides, it looks like the washing powder under our sink at home, which we have enough of.

Cemile's friends on bikes are quiet ones. They seem to be more fussed about playing detective around the farm. We avoid the burnt-out cars and man standing in the car park. There's a door blocked by a massive steel bin, big as a bed. We wheel it to the left and go into the room where there's live electrics crackling. Double plug sockets running up the wall, ten dual plug sockets many up the wall.

White cabling on the floor opened up and stretched down into the hole left behind from a lifted-out felt tile. All the square tiles around it make it look like a puzzle room with the square tiles slowly disappearing in a timed bonus mode. We hop from square tile to square tile, trying not to fall through into the wire holes. In an arcade game I would lose, this is probably why I never go to a party at Rowan's Bowling with Angela. Some people at school say it's cos my mum can't afford it, but Angela said her mum would pay.

We've let the rain in with us and so the little felt tiles are covered in our footprints, but they're not disappearing. The mud tracks embarrass me too.

Would I treat my own home like this?

As we pull away on the bike I look at the mural, bigger than my house. All the rain coming off the walls of Debden block sounding like the painted waterfall is coming alive. All we're missing is the sound of birds, I'm wondering whether they all went away one winter and never came back. The waterfall rocks are grey to clash with the farm in its oranges and lilacs, trees peep out from the painting just the same way they peep out around the blocks.

Cemile's aunt sees us from her window and next minute we're in her home. Lace covers all the cupboards here, like in mine. Go straight to the kitchen and help Cemile carry some snacks out. Here this curly girl properly meets me, watching if I like the same biscuits as her and how I react to her deyze's gossip. Is her dad still being horrible to her sister? She tells me about Filiz, how she had bad bruises but they've gone now so it's OK. *Turkish Cypriot*

As we leave we duck our heads under a plant hanging above the door. The stairs down seem to go on too long, I worry we're going underground into the magma in the middle of the earth but then we come through, back up to biking.

Cemile had so much freedom. Her sister gave her ways out. Not all of us lived so lucky lucky.

DAMLA: TOTTENHAM'S PLUMBING, MARCH 2000

Anne has been quiet for too long. Always going on about cabbages. My neighbour is pulling out all of the grass in his garden so he can pour concrete down and make sure no foxes and rabbits get in. The slats in our fence look at me, ready to be dragged apart.

Today Topuz Paşa walks in with Cemile and he wants to jumble up who goes where.

—All right, kids, you leave us in peace, Mehmet abi is going to take you to play computer games at his.

Nene is sleeping because her medication has her that way. If she was awake I would be staying at home. İpek and Erhan are too small for this. We need to go in pairs. Zade can take the little ones and Mehmet abi can take me. And Cemile. Who seems to be frustrated that we are split off in this way. She likes Zade. The few times we have met her she has done crosswords with Zade. Smart woman. My mum only wants to make friends if they're smart. I tell Cemile this and she gets angry and accuses Anne of not being friends with her mum Tulay, which means that Anne must think her mum is dumb. Nobody has a dumb mum. Zade arrives and is flattered because all she catches is that she is a smart woman.

When Mehmet abi pulls up, his car smells of this spray bottle he keeps called 'car cologne'. He spritzes up the passenger seat before I sit down. Why didn't Cemile sit next to him? Is he not her second dad? We are treating him like a taxi. His hand reaches back through the gap next to the driver's seat to reach her knee at the back. With a smack, they begin a game they know. She tries to tuck her knees close to the soft of the seat to avoid his hand, while he is waving about at the back trying to smack her. In tights today, Cemile is angry that his fingernail has snagged them.

What a nice house he has. All one floor but pictures everywhere because he is a proud kind of man. Cemile is on his walls with her sister, who looks like a tweezer-happy version of her. Topuz Paşa is there as a boy. There's another little girl in a dress, long like a wedding one. That's his god-daughter and ex's niece. Mehmet abi says he knows my dad and that they were like best friends until he moved into a bedsit with some boy in a dress putting thinking in his head. Why isn't my dad on the wall too, then? Or me?

All the new games are under a chair towering with unfolded clothes. If we had our mums here they'd probably poke us to help Mehmet abi. They might even make a comment about the girl who is here all the time or in the cafe, Agata. Agata with the niece on Mehmet abi's wall, Agata who is not Mehmet abi's wife but comes to the man's house and doesn't dust the top of his cupboard – she might only wipe the inside of the kitchen cupboards once before the rims of glasses and cups touch the laminate wood.

Sandwiches first.

They're weird because he has put pork in them and we don't

eat pork but we eat them because when you don't eat something for a long time then you want it.

Backbread? That's the best bit. You get the most bread from that bit.

We swap sandwiches but the level of bread has equalled out because she took a bite so I don't have the most bread. Backbread tastes better if you:

1. Chew it all up.
2. Hold it on your tongue until it goes to mush.
3. Spit it out into your hand.
4. Mould it into a dough cake (I do squares).
5. Pat, pat and pull.

It's almost like you get to eat both lunch and dessert, two foods in one. It doesn't make sense to me why people would find that disgusting. When I look up to see, Agata has come by the flat and is grossed out by me with my cake in my palm. Minus ten points.

She asks how Cemile's sister is doing. Asks a bit too much and brings Cemile's back up. It's not like Agata is family to ask. We have a bit of attitude, Mehmet abi thinks, with all the backbread and quietness around strangers. There's knocking at his front door and I feel we're nearly ten, us two curious girls moving our heads same-time towards the sound.

We're asked to go to his room and sit down on his bed while the PlayStation gets set up, and a charger pokes me from under the covers. The start-up sound also sounds like me saying 'ow' and Mehmet abi agrees, so sings it out.

—Zzzzowwww.

We make him smile. When he is tired at home, sometimes he turns it on and off because he likes the sound and now he will remember us when he does that. Especially if he is sad tired, turning the computer on and off.

Driplets from the screen and a man
standing in a car park.
It looks a bit like the one under Tangmere.

When the man on the screen walks, his shoes clip-clop. All these cars and he finally picks one, gets in it and starts to drive off. I don't think the car is his because police pop up and try to ram him out the car park and in car parks like this there are a lot of sneaky corners so he knows his way out of those tight spaces. He drives off with the police behind him. Driver.

Cemile isn't happy, she's played this one before. He didn't save her file but I get to play it for the first time. The controller gets passed straight to me – how do I get the car out? We play until I start to get real sleepy, red eyes. Mehmet abi comes back in later. Real sleepy, red eyes.

We can go soon! The time was starting to feel hard to put a pin in, you need to know when things are gonna be done otherwise everything is mush. It's about 4 a.m.

Sideways stepping past us, Mehmet abi leans forward over his bedside table tap-tapping, and his shirt rises up to show a mat of hair on his lower back. I look at his boxers, which are blue with a red border, and cannot stop wanting to yank them down. It is not that I want to look at his bum. I want to hit it with something, it feels as though he is leaning forward like this and he is doing it so someone can get at him. I have to hold onto the arm of the couch so hard. It feels like a dog's paw, which is the only thing that gets me to stop thinking about his boxers and the pullable, grabbable material. Zade used to have a dog until it got put down for being the wrong breed. It was a nice dog and we used to have a connection.

Keys clink and the PlayStation goes off. When we come out of his bedroom, Agata is waiting to walk us home, but we refuse because we want to go in the car and our mums didn't say we could walk with her. Better to walk alone. Cemile reminds Mehmet abi that her dad wanted to talk to him anyway, and the thought of Ufuk abi gets him agreeing to take us on the ten-minute car ride to mine.

If life was a computer game, this moment would be where the screen freezes and then the glitch ends as the car you were driving suddenly has four police cars hovering on top of it as it slides into a pixelated tree.

The entrance to Mehmet abi's flat has a double door for security. First the iron gate and then the normal wood one. Outside an English man is screaming that they're about to come in if we don't open the door fast, but instead of opening the door, Mehmet abi is running past us to get back into the bedroom.

They give five seconds. We hear a sawing through the iron gate. Whatever is sawing through the gate door is quick at its job and I can feel it in the air when it finally cuts through enough for them to step through to the next part. From the bedside table, Mehmet abi has grabbed something. Across the corridor is the bathroom and we follow him as he runs to the toilet and tips powder into it, and after tipping, he tries to flush but the flush in this old flat has always been a problem flush, which is why the toilet paper from when I did a number one is still there as a pillow to the powder, gently holding it up so it looks fresh except for the bits of water in it. Flush flush. It is as though the whole house is groaning with us, trying to get the powder to go down. The pipes aren't having it until eventually they do, about one minute before the saw coming through the iron gate.

As if a bomb has gone off, the wood door comes right off and Agata is screaming, louder than I ever thought she could go.

—It's all right, we'll replace the door, miss.

Down the stairs are lots of men with guns and they come in, barging Mehmet abi as he comes out the bathroom with his hands up. Cemile winks at me as she puts something in her pocket and it is probably that she has seen this big amount of men with guns already. There's no cash in the flat that he can't explain. Evidence gets taken till 10 a.m. Cuffs come out for Mehmet abi. They find money that Mehmet abi says is from selling shearling jackets, and he shows the leftover jackets in his cupboard. When they eventually take him off without much fuss, Agata promises us that it's no big deal, he's come through worse. They've been tabbing the area for a while now and all sorts of strangers got photoed coming in and out of Mehmet abi's house, but that's all they have. Apparently this is Operation Haddock and the entire area has been getting swept all day. The only major find of the day is a long-reach machete. The plumbing in Tottenham is slow but does its job. Every toilet in this part of town must be rich.

One of the policemen is holding Agata's elbow and asks her if she's single. Cemile and me laugh. She points at her god-daughter on the wall and says that's her baby. He doesn't ask her any more questions.

The officers – who ask what we're doing here – pull us to the side and keep us talking about PlayStation until a woman comes over to us. Agata gets told that it's OK for her to leave us with them and actually they have everything they need from her, so she goes. The lady introduces herself to us as a social worker and it's surprising how friendly she is for no reason.

She has a colleague with her. Cemile goes off in one car. I go in another. Why was I at Mehmet abi's house? I explain the PlayStation again, and how Anne won't buy me one. In her car she takes me up Philip Lane past the launderette. This launderette has been here since she was a little girl apparently, but the social worker's husband won't believe her, he thinks it's only been there about five years. According to her, you replace memories with fake ones if you're not careful. Like your brain is lying to you. Sometimes we turn our memories inside out to block out the truth, and she wonders whether I do this, whether I twist up my thinking to say things how I think I should say things.

My memories go back a long time, I feel like I remember everything, even from when I was little little.

We all change our memories sometimes. There are some memories, she says, that are so important to you it doesn't matter if they're true or not. The launderette, for example, she remembers when all the blue metal letters on the store front spelt out 'launderette' and she remembers that being when she was in her twenties, which she is far from now. She has this story of a fire that happened there, which her husband doesn't believe either. It would have been about eighteen years ago, and it was these bed linens covered in massage oil, absolutely drenched they must have been. If you shove your linens into the dryer after they've been washed, shove them so they're piled in together in folds and stacks, then you don't allow the heat to dissipate properly. It makes sense to think that there was a fire there, because you can see these big smoky patches behind the machines where the walls probably never got cleaned properly. Social worker husband still thinks that's silly, if there'd been a fire, they would have done a proper refurb job, you wouldn't see smoke patches. They've both been meaning to stop in at the launderette to see who's telling the truth, it's important not to leave the truth up in the air. The two of them have been worried about whether this is confabulation, an example of her getting dementia.

It's at this point that she comes to a pause outside my house and turns to me from the driver's seat. Do I know why it took Mehmet abi so long to open the door? If I concentrate properly, is there a memory somewhere?

Lining my neighbour's front window are porcelain babies. Most of them are belly down but smiling up at visitors. They all have little boob creases and wear off-the-shoulder dresses. One baby has hair with the sides shaved, sticking up like a punk's, and has its finger to its lips. He's chosen mostly ginger ones with blue eyes and uses them to weight down his curtains so they stay open. If I concentrate properly, is there a memory somewhere? From the inside of his house, he is smiling at me. He is sitting in an armchair. A granddad chair, he is small in comparison. As I shake my head at the social worker lady, he thinks I am shaking it at him maybe, because he is laughing. I swear this man is always either laughing or angry. Small man laughing, it's as though I can hear him from the car. I want to talk to the lady now about other memories but he stops laughing almost as soon as I think the thought. The way his eyes catch me from there, I know not to talk too much.

Social worker lady brings me to my front door and waits for me to get my keys out; once we're inside she stays quiet and I do too. The front door barely clicks as it shuts. Anne and Topuz Paşa are there with papers around them in the sitting room. Some of them have the most beautiful drawings of cabbage, like something out of an old recipe book. Anne has always had the most delicate hands, when she draws she barely seems to hold the pen.

He tries at her, hands going to her leg. She laughs and I cannot laugh. I find myself suspicious. If Topuz Paşa sees me, he'll know that I know he was rejected. Maybe his looking at me while I'm looking will make me lose all of my teeth. Something like if you have an evil face and the wind changes, your face will stay like that. People can fix you into one place with one look, so you have to be careful.

She didn't smile until she put his hand far away from her. I think of him like a spinning top, swivelling away as she sends him off in another direction. My mum is good like that; she makes it easy for me to love life. Life where you can play it like a pinball machine, sending those hands away. Men are like these tiny balls always on a slant, rolling towards you. The rest of us swerve and bat. Anne has spotted us standing there and she calls me over, parades her motherhood as if it were a chastity belt – hugs me loudly, hides her face in my shoulder. Topuz Paşa looks at me with nice on his face, his look is a relief to me. He doesn't know that I know. I keep my tongue holding my teeth firmly in place.

Social worker lady has been taking everything in. She asks Anne all the same questions that she asked me. Says that I seem withdrawn and she should get me to talk more. I tell her Nene keeps me talking all the time; you should see the two of us. Social worker lady asks to meet her so we take her to the downstairs bedroom where Nene is watching her romance TV. I'm loud in my shock when she spoilers *Deli Yürek* for me and tells me that Zeynep has gotten jealous with Yusuf and told him to go fudge himself. In the middle of this disaster, the social worker lady has left. She'll come back.

Topuz Paşa high-fives me for the television routine and then leaves the house in a rush. How come? From her bed, Nene looks bigger than usual, her feet swollen and hot-looking. We're still waiting for Zade to get back. There's a picture of me sitting by a pile of pruned branches with Erhan and İpek – the three of us in the garden in the summer, smiling. Outside now, the sun is coming through clear as rush hour begins. The three of us hold hands and watch the show.

TOPUZ PAŞA, SPRING 2000
BEFORE THE DRIVE

I'm driving out of Istanbul and look behind me to the far horizon, stretching all the way back to a plot of cabbages. They circle the horizon, looking like mould in a toenail, the cream of built-up apartments stretching further than a dot of calcium on the nail. There is a man rolling beside my lorry on a stretcher (through the middle of the road) and the traffic attendant is giving him a heart bypass. He is awake through the procedure and palms his forehead like my disappointed mother, 'Oh, why do you have to do that for, be?'[oi] Instead of blood gushing out of him, he is seeping with near-clear juices. I worry they are from my pickled cabbages, that I should have transported my goods using some other method. I check the back window and there are stacks of pickles gently knocking as I drive and this is why I asked for someone to source me a truck. No . . . not a truck, a people carrier. I hop out of the car and try to catch every drop from his body in the jars that I keep in my numerous pockets.

I stress dream. I have this cyst on my groin and it's been a cheeky one to wake up to. Too cheeky for me to have anyone come look at it, and by anyone the last person I mean is the doctor. I think that if I stick around for long enough that she

Turkish Cypriot

will – eventually – get bored of being a single mum. Imagine the timing of it, if the one day she does consider having a peek under my trousers she's got this big boy of a cyst eyeballing her back? When I dream (if they are those kind of dreams), I end up pinching the cyst in my sleep, trying to make it clear off and leak out before the best bit of the dream.

Ayla has boring at the back of her eyes. All that spirit about her and everything spicy she says, she says it with a bit of sex. That doesn't stop me seeing that she's making an ask for routine, right around the reflection in the corner of her right and left. Them eyes!

There's nothing in the world that makes me feel more human than sex. If I really calculate everything I've done for myself and for other people, there has been motivation there, always gunning for one thing. What I love most of all is sexual routine. I love it when we think it has become boring. There you are, two people, tired and lying on each other like village dogs as though the only way out of the slowness is through each other. That's why we say 'pillow talk', why we say 'getting lost in each other'.

I have a friend who moved to Vietnam recently. He cashed up everything he could from his place in Dalston and just went over there to get himself a nice cheap house with a woman included. His brother was there before him and has set himself up with this new factory – totally in-your-face sweatshop. He calls himself a business owner and everyone recognises him in Saigon. Vietnam's apparel industry is thriving, I hear. Memo would be having the time of his life out there with his shearling jackets. Everything is to gain out there. The factories are kitted up Stoke Newington-style, pilling and snagging testers, cutting plotters and bobbin winders. Now the Turks out there are making money from selling non-toxic chemicals for organic cotton and wetting agents for your jeans to cut down dyeing time and energy. I can just picture Mehmet now with his swatches of spandex and jacquard. On Sundays, my friend's brother plays golf and then goes home to ring his kids for an hour. That's a life, imagine cashing in on something that doesn't have your back out 24/7. I need to check if my car's got insurance for this drive.

Approaching Romania there's a warm spell and weather forecasts tell the public about synoptic conditions of unexpected heat. This is a comparably hot period for March, Şeytan is dancing for the drug smugglers. By the time Topuz Paşa pulls up, the cabbages in his bright green lorry are rotting. McDonald's is in his head again. He says to himself, 'This is why burger flippers are making more money than me.' The problem with success for men like him is often gambling or gogo. Actually, Mehmet loves both gambling and gogo. Topuz Paşa is tired of barriers to access. Smugglers need to inform to avoid arrest. Snitching is most common when a smuggler has arrived back in London and is looking to get involved with eyes on the street-style work. They take the attention they've had from police off their backs and pass it over to someone else. It is unfair really. There are men around Green Lanes who have so many properties of their own, they've been whispering in Polis Bey's $_{Policeman's}^{Mr}$ ear for the entirety of their careers. Topuz Paşa would prefer not to get other people arrested. He knows about the wires that Babo keeps in his house, and feels a sense of dread. The torturers never even sterilise their clips and pricks.

At the East Turkey border it is easy for him. He did his askerlik *military service*
with one of the men who lets him through. His load is just
some cabbage after all. Through coffee shop banter, he has
often heard about officers who will put eroin in the back of
trucks for dealers after getting paid off. Based on this precon-
ception, he thought it would be easier for him to get the cabbages
through. But he still has to bargain in a sweating shirt. The
March of his crossing happens to clash with a month of poor
ozone; a load of soldiers stand, miserable in their uniforms.
The soldiers have been subject to random searches from the
police. They respond in kind, stopping and searching the police
on occasion, but the toing and froing has become tiring. They
ask him about the English writing on his vehicle and argue
that exporting vegetables during March means that you are
taking money out of the country for the benefit of a British
company. The problem stays with the vegetables and the pos-
sibility of drug smuggling is not really entertained. Topuz Paşa
doesn't have to use his pitch to the border man, the one about
how Babo's kilos of eroin are just a pile of tomato tins in a
room full of canned goods. A localised scrap in a stable market.

Topuz Paşa focuses instead on the Balkans, they don't
have enough cabbage compared to the other exporters. Most
cabbages exported out of Turkey end up in pickle, but not
this cabbage. It's in the best interest of the culture to share
cabbage in its organic form, Topuz Paşa thinks. Plus, the rate
of cabbages being exported is fairly low when you consider
that the entirety of the product can fit into a single lorry.

It is a shame that after the hold-up at the Turkish border,
the cabbages are found to be rotting. Despite the fact that the
cabbages grown in Turkey were intermixed with onion in the

soil, the implantation of the heroin bags was too clumsy and rough-handed. They had spoilt the product. The cabbages have been through a lot. Topuz Paşa is angry. He swings topuz up and down in the air when he needs to calm down. It's a cheap staff that he swaps out with whatever is to hand. He gets out of his lorry and takes out his frustration in this way. The staff is new, a carob branch whittled down by a Bulgarian man he met on his journey. Up and down the staff goes, until his arms are tired enough for his head to think clearly.

Among the cabbages in his lorry there are dummy ones too, they are just standard without anything inside them. At the Romanian border he asks the officials to direct him to the hungriest people in Cenad, the closest village. He gestures at the rotting cabbages that he needs to shift before he reaches England. Mardin Din Din want to be the best vegetable importers in the West but are still struggling to establish themselves in an overcrowded market. This has meant that the quality checks back at their farm in Mardin are not always thorough. In Cenad, Topuz Paşa is free of border patrol and desperately trades his dummy cabbages for sarma until his stomach is full and his load is lighter. He takes it to heart every time one of his standard cabbages receives a compliment.

If he does this again, there are calculations to be made. Better risk assessments and weighing the cons with a sharper set of eyes. The moment he gets back to England he explains this to Babo, who finds him disrespectful and slightly irresponsible. Topuz Paşa's payment is about three months away and dependent on how much Babo's eighty sells for.

When he tells Ayla that most of the cabbages were rotten by the time he reached England, she laughs.

SUPERMARKET ACADEMIC,
APRIL 2000

Nehir supermarket has been closed down. The old man who kept it running without ever leaving his stool has retired. The vegetables haven't been restocked for months. Inside are boxes of cigarettes that nobody's going to sell under the counter any more. Nehir supermarket was named after a river, and in the spirit of a river it has had to change its course pretty quick. Now, it has the smell of switched-off freezer when Ayla and Topuz Paşa walk in. Damp and defrosting. A film of dust covers everything, but that was the same when it was open to the public. Topuz Paşa opens a packet of crisps from a black bag propped up against crates of beans by his feet. The crisps are already squashed bits so eating is tipping into mouth. Ayla's eyes follow the crumbs as if for pure entertainment. They both sit on blue vats of Super Mastic, unsold, like most of the contents of Nehir.

Topuz Paşa: I've done everything else for you. I've done with the half-ounces, I got customers now – this is the low end – the dangerous end. Time for our easy sales with posh boys. The amount of money you get for three little bags or so . . . these guys love it. We'll give their buyers two ounces for £1,400. They'll nearly double that by selling it in grams.

Ayla: Where are you thinking of doing it?

Topuz Paşa: Up in Muswell Hill. Camden Town. Bloomsbury. Oh, by the way, the amount who use it in the city is unbelievable.

Ayla: That doesn't sound so hard to believe, except for how they get away with it.

Topuz Paşa: Drink methadone for one week – slow slow slow and everything is perfect. Don't think too much, I go in, get our money, go out. How's my outfit?

Sky blue for the pinstriped suit. Coral for the shirt. Topuz Paşa keeps a uniform for his upmarket work. He irons it about twice a year. This morning, from a cupboard filled with mothballs and bags of lavender, he took his suit out of its dry-cleaning bag and got ready for the day. He's unlike Mehmet and does not douse himself in cologne for special occasions, instead a quick bit of deodorant and minimal hair oil. Ayla has known another man who wore suits and wore them well; three-piece suits with polished shoes and thumb-curled hair.

Ayla: Bit colourful.

Topuz Paşa: Thank you! Come in the car, come with me, it's good to have company and yeah, you'll like Muswell Hill.

As they drive at night out past Wood Green, the whole area has begun to take another life. Through the car windows, Topuz Paşa lets in the smell of lamb doner until the two realise they haven't eaten a proper meal. It is the last time Ayla will be involved like this with this messy business. How to celebrate?

They pull up with hazard lights on; Topuz Paşa gets out to buy two durum wraps for them, eating as he drives until the inevitable. Chilli sauce staining his left knee, he pours water over his leg until something closer to blue comes peeking from the oil. When he reaches Elms Avenue, they see people smoking by the front door. So many of the group are wearing suit jackets and boot-cut jeans that Ayla smirks to herself; posh people always like to dress half-smart for parties when they have the money for smart. Not one person dressed in a recognisable cut.

Topuz Paşa: I know what you're thinking. Just because they're doctors doesn't mean they have any money, these are the ones who study dead writers, not surgeons who change up your whole face.

They park opposite the house. The house has a brick-built outbuilding and this seems to be where most of the human traffic is coming from. Whenever people open the door to leave the outbuilding, they hear different music from the soft lo-fi that can be heard playing from the main house. Topuz Paşa goes to the door, waiting with his fingers in his belt like a cowboy. Ayla tops up her wrap with red cabbage.

AYLA, SAME DAY

Topuz Paşa gets back into the car and explains to me that the buyer was spooked when he approached the front door; they would prefer someone less shifty to invite inside for the exchange. They wouldn't even open the door. His suit was too colourful. Or maybe it was the stain from the durum. He promises me that I won't be at risk. I know I will be at risk but the key thing is that I don't show it. I have to put words like risk and kids out of my head. Topuz Paşa thinks there's something about a woman that makes it easier for these people to open the door. A woman who has enough that's familiar about her to spell out safe. The reification of moral trade, me in my dress, for example, no longer looks like a business transaction. This'll be a one-off. A business experience.

If the children's father were here, he would be going in with a briefcase in one hand and his sunglasses in the other. He'd have the same confidence that he picks the kids up with. His clothes wouldn't look like fancy dress. I need to morph into him and smarten up. Hasan Buli, the outlaw who hid in the Kıbrıs mountains from authorities, wore his lover's clothes to slip away into darkness. That's me. In the car, the leather seats seem to be elevating me and propelling me out of my seat. I take the package from Topuz Paşa and the takeaway wrappers too. There are crates outside the house where people throw their things and I chuck the polystyrene boxes into one of them. Then I pause for a moment and smooth down the lining of my dress, and straighten its pockets. From the window two people in their early thirties are nudging each other, one in a bucket hat.

The latch on the front gate won't give until I put some back into it, and then it swings open so fast I nearly fall over with it. I can feel men watching me and I really wish I was in my lover's clothes – a suit, covered by a blanket . . . As I walk towards the front door, party smokers move out of the way but still joke in my direction. My ears are out for their jokes – if they're aimed at me or just heard by me. By the time I am at the door it is already open, and would you believe it? I'm greeted by someone I recognise from their taste in art, to whom all the paintings under my lover's bed belonged at one point.

—I know you!

AYLA SHAKING HANDS

Ayla looks up at pure height in a skirt and belly top, the word 'you' stretching out so that it stands alone as an exclamation of surprise. Bucket Hat offers his hand to Ayla. She barely shakes it, her focus completely on Eric.

Eric: She used to come to my little bedsit. How's your Romeo doing?

Sometimes when Ayla is stressed she notices herself salivating. She takes a pause to suck all the saliva out of her mouth before she clears her throat and answers.

Ayla: He's fine, getting a lot of reading done in jail, as you can imagine. Have you been to visit him?

Eric: No! Why would I? I wouldn't want someone seeing me like that if it were me. When he's out.

Eric shrugs gentle. Looking closer, their clothes seem more frayed than she'd have expected from them, and their posture less assured. Eric turns to Bucket Hat and back again to Ayla.

Eric: Ah, sorry, this is my friend Neil . . . I guess we met in Cagliari, right? At a rambling festival but as part of a group of writers who had been invited. I was brought in to talk about Baudelaire, flâneur and the like. Whoever popped the two of us on that events programme must have been an absolute fire-starter. There are all these progressive ideas in the art

world and you end up slotting what you know into a gap –
and that's it. Not much to it. It's as though it's some kind of
shamanic show rather than a genuine gesture of furthering
the discussion.

She looks at them, waiting for the rubbish to finish, before
shaking Bucket Hat's hand again and turning back to Eric.

Bucket Hat (out of breath): My concern is exactly the same.
It's a literary concern, and that hasn't changed.

While they speak Ayla has started to edge towards a door
to her right, it is ajar to show a box room that's empty except
for an exercise bike with the words 'BodyMAX' across the
flywheel. She is looking at her phone as messages from Topuz
Paşa start to arrive.

Topuz Paşa
10-Apr-2000 22:34
You taking toilet or sutn?

OPTIONS   REPLY   BACK

Topuz Paşa
10-Apr-2000 22:38
Stop flirting! ;-)

OPTIONS   REPLY   BACK

Topuz Paşa
10-Apr-2000 22:45   *I'm gonna come!*
Want me to bring tea in for you? Gelecem!

OPTIONS   REPLY   BACK

---

*Turkish
Cypriot*

Ayla: I haven't got much time, I need to get back to my kids. Can we do this now? In that room?

Eric has already slipped into the box room, and leans against the bike waiting for Ayla to join him.

Bucket hat: Oh, I'm really looking forward to this. I'm only upset you're not a gogo dancer like your friend on the phone promised. You would be great!

Ayla: Gogo means cocaine. He didn't mean a woman going going for it.

Bucket Hat puts his hands over his hat like a football manager at a game.

Bucket Hat: Well that just goes to show that when you do things in an art context you have the satisfaction of no satisfaction at all.

Ayla (with vim): OK, it's time for the money now; you forget other people have places to go despite your important literary enquiry. I've got a car waiting for me outside.

As though Topuz Paşa can sense her words, his car horn beeps to the Gunners theme tune. Bucket Hat instinctively fumbles for his plastic sleeve in his back pocket before shaking it at the window, then passes it to Ayla in the box room. She counts it in front of him before giving him the drugs in a heavily taped black bag.

Bucket Hat: Lovely. All the physical arcana of the heroin trade attract me more than the mutational possibilities of it, if you ask me.

Eric: Nobody asked you, though. OK, miss, give the kids a hello from me, they must remember me from your belly.

Ayla: You've only seen me pregnant once, I think. Home is all in your imagination, my friend.

Eric: The moment I read Perec I was fucked. If you haven't got it, you've got to somehow perform the possibilities of home, and art becomes the space in which to do this.

Ayla: You're one of those people who think too much and then wonder why you're not happy.

Eric is the only one not laughing at this. The car bibs again and the attention it is attracting has alarmed Ayla. A lift of the eyebrow does what a shrug would do, and Ayla nods her head goodbye. Eric asks to keep in touch. On her way to the gate, Bucket Hat follows her. Topuz Paşa steps out of the car.

Bucket: Excuse me, can I have your number before you go?

Shaking her head, Ayla is then tapped on the elbow by Topuz Paşa to guide her back into the car. She swerves his touch, jumps in herself, and turns up the volume of Londra Türk Radyosu. Eric ushers Bucket Hat back inside to talk about the ghettoisation of academia and the need for self-reflexivity in gaining public interest, to sniff heroin, and to linger on the eleven possible digits of Ayla's number.

AYLA, SCHOOL RUN, 2000

I'm on the school run for Zade too today. My friend's little one is in the same year as Erhan, his name is Warren and he's got so much energy that I have to rush all the kids so we stay at the same pace.

We're going to have a party at his mum's house. I send the kids ahead of me to walk up the stairs to get to her door, narrow, not too long, not too far. Then I look through the letterbox to see if it's hers because I always get the doors mixed up. In the one metre from the letterbox I recognise an overload of children's shoes, storage boxes, bags and umbrellas where everything that can't fit goes. A little see-through zipper bag from Bruce Grove Nursery for her little boy, he must have forgotten it. On the phone, I can hear Zade shouting at someone while she's chopping something, I think. Damla interrupts me to ring the doorbell.

By the time Zade has reached the door she is happy, a cuddle before smiling us over to the kitchen. The kitchen smells like cinnamon and nutmeg. Flooding out from the bin are carrot peelings. From whisky tumblers she passes me a drink thick with condensed milk, with a kick. She's added spiced carrot and ginger iced juice to a good few shots of rum, shaking extra egg over the top like pepper. The table has drinks all over it so I single out Super T for later, and a huge bottle of Vimto for the kids.

She's what some people would call OTT with cleaning, but perfect to me. Very clean. Always washes her dishes with gloves on, and always wraps her hair in a bandana to cook. Prawn, rice and jerk chicken with reheated dolma I've brought over, all to be on the same plate. A slow cook, we kill time with carrot juice at the kitchen table. The kids run straight to the bedroom, though, and I can hear they've already started to jump on the bed. Screams every now and then when one falls off.

Lovers' rock plays from a cassette player, Beres Hammond to Louisa Mark. A selection for every mood collected over the decades, barely a tape goes to waste. Side by side, we do the cooking and the cheersing dance, wining towards the dustbin to chuck garlic peel, twirling around each other until time eats itself up. We don't talk about shouting that happens over the phone or people who wear bucket hats, we just dance. She gives me a plate to bring back for my mum to have something to eat, and a big water bottle of carrot juice without the rum to take home, telling me to add that in later.

DAMLA, SAME DAY
AT ZADE'S, 2000

İpek always wants me to be her big sister and forgets that I am not so big. She wants me to put her on my back and jump on the bed but she is so heavy that I jump now and she falls with me. The bed's mattress is too small for the wooden base, and when I fall I hit my tailbone so hard that I feel a pain go up my entire back. We play hide-and-seek in this flat because it's harder here, the smaller the place the more difficult the game is. Erhan and Warren are hiding so long because I have left them. Me and İpek can hear them giggling because they think they have found the best hiding place, but actually we are taking the time to put their toys away so that when they come out it will look like nobody is here. It's all good until Erhan comes out and his eyes are big and betrayed-looking. From the landing, we can hear someone who thinks that this flat is their flat and they're jamming their keys in the door but not getting in. I watch İpek go to the letterbox and open it to look through at him and the man looks back at her, then at me after I join. He is so old that his neck skin is another pair of ears. When he shuffles away, he swears at us and the word is so bad that I have to explain what it means to İpek. Our mums are laughing in the kitchen, and we don't tell them about this.

AN UPDATE ON NEHIR
SUPERMARKET, 2000

Nehir supermarket has had a change of owners. The family who have bought it enjoy its easy links to a couple of train stations and its proximity to a wholesaler who they are also related to. They like the name, so keep it. Nehir for newness, water always washing rocks in a riverbed so detritus doesn't settle. Before, Sadi had not made the most of the space. He supervised and did the occasional veg run but there was no real expertise in his selections. Watermelons were always bought past the point of ripeness, and the only stock that got bought up was tobacco and its bottled friends. The new family who have bought it have invested in signs that bring people in. Nehir now promises continental food spanning sauerkraut to crates of raw green almond. The father of the new family styles himself in polo shirts and pocketed army shorts, and drives every three days to refresh his veg with the bakers in between. He has a daughter Erhan's age, and expects to find a boy who will help him in the shop straight out of school. Standing at the counter and spending less than you make is a skill in this area, and the new family have this.

DAMLA, WALKING PAST NEHIR, SUMMER 2000

Cemile has İpek holding her hand after only a few visits. She comes to knock for me and Anne says we can go anywhere as long as we take İpek. There's a park we want to go to where the swings are less rusted. On the way, you go by Nehir and it stands out now more than it did when Sadi abi looked after it. On the big new sign they have, I want to get the fresh bread and I want to eat sandwiches with Cemile again like we did at Mehmet abi's. If it's Turkish pide, it's all basically backbread flattened out just how I like it but I'm not sure if Cemile eats Turkish bread. Probably. Her mum is a properly Turkish mum who always smells like food and never turns up at my house without something baked. This is maybe why we don't visit her mum so much, Anne and I; we always have to make something to go there.

İpek is impatient with me, she wants everything that we walk past and runs straight into the post office when I tell her not to. It's as if she forgets that when we looked everywhere for loose coins this morning (even under Anne's shoes), there was nothing there. If it's not chocolate she asks for, it's something that doesn't even exist, like a block of rainbow cheese. İpek promises me that she saw rainbow cheese on TV once.

She is making Cemile laugh, which makes me laugh, so I am not so unhappy that we are babysitting her. At school, a man came in to teach us how to drum and that made Cemile laugh, so it made me laugh too. She is laughing more now than I've ever noticed before. İpek is walking almost crouching to the floor, with her belly sticking out. Guilt is all over her face and eventually a Barbie toothbrush falls out onto the floor by Bruce Grove station. We did notice her looking at the toothbrush and how she spun the rack it was on for too long but of all the things she could of stolen, she stole the any-day thing. The toothbrush gets snatched out of her hand so that she can learn that she was wrong. Little hands jab at my sides until I return the toothbrush, and I wonder how wrong it is really. Nobody will miss that toothbrush.

Cemile talks too much around my little sister but I don't mind. She has just turned ten and is thinking it's time for a first kiss to come. We can see from our approach to the small park by Nehir that her sister Filiz is having her seven thousandth kiss with the boy who sometimes hangs around Mehmet abi, and smells of his house. They are kissing too much to get away with it! I have to distract İpek so she leaves them alone. There is a bigness coming over Cemile as she spies on them from the electricity bin that we've ducked behind. Arj passes Filiz a cigarette and I can smell the oregano in it from four skips away. Another couple come out of the lido drained of water. Little sis thinks that they've come out of nowhere until I lift her up a little bit to see they came from the hole in the ground. We're noticed. Cemile takes my hand softly softly. They finish their cigarettes before coming towards us. Filiz's face is so blissful, she doesn't bother telling us to go home. Daylight has started to fade out and the moment is nearly completely stress-free. As Filiz comes eye to eye with Cemile, a frown quickly cuts through the calm. Something goes between the sisters; when Filiz crosses the pavement and jumps into a tinted-out jeep with Arj, her little sister turns to me and tells me not to tell my mum I saw those two together, or she'll tell her about İpek's toothbrush. Anne would find the toothbrush story funny but now's not the time to push things, Cemile doesn't need to lay it all out for me to be reminded of secrets and Ufuk abi's parenting.

When we come into the park, it's almost empty except for men meeting at benches for long debates. The kids' park is further in and when we get there, boys our age sit and scratch shapes into the wooden house above the slide. This may be why Cemile likes bringing İpek out. Any excuse to come places like this. Cemile gets the same way about going swimming with us too. Tumbling her into the floor, Cemile tickles İpek and brings attention to us. Maybe this is a try at making it into the wooden bit with the boys, for a kiss in real life, or in legend, her name scratched into the wall. Even better because they're from outside school. When we see people from another school, we don't say hello – we just do this until we get a hello. The attention campaign carries on until İpek's up high on a swing. We're pushing İpek so far, her screams are not so happy. I don't know why we ignore her begging us to stop pushing the swing so hard and we're about to stop but it's too late and she's gone properly flying. I run to go to her and she has little black rocks over her face and is asleep. Cemile tells me that I've knocked my sister out and calls me an idiot for the first time. I slap İpek and she wakes up telling me that she was dreaming she was on a big ice slide trying to chase down a stick of gum. The boys cuss us, jump down from the top and walk away without acknowledging Cemile. Her nose flares. I feel happy. I'm lost in their shadow, Cemile watching them leave until they are only small.

GAMING WITH FILIZ,
SUMMER OF 2000

Al elmaya taş atan çok olur: no enemies is a sign that fortune
has forgotten you.

Cemile and I are reminded of this by her sister. Filiz thinks
she's blessed us with the little bit of time she's put in with us
this evening. We know this because she is doing her best to
school us on things when we're just trying to play *Majora's
Mask* on Cemile's Nintendo 64.

> Moon Child wearing a fish mask
> —Initiate conversation with NPC?
> Cue: 'Does the right thing really make everybody happy?'

The right thing? Filiz leans in towards the screen where Moon
Child speaks, and laughs because the character has proven
her point. You have to do the right thing even if you upset
some people sometimes. She knows she will upset a lot of
people when they find out who she's seeing but there's no
point making a big drama out of relationships, you just have
to go with who you want. Arjîn was the first person to offer
her a lift to Central without her having to get the train, and
he had no problems paying for parking.

Filiz is sure of the fact that it shouldn't be set out from birth who you grow up to fall in love with. This love that she talks about feels a bit less powerful than expected, considering how much her family are going to be raging about it. But me and Cemile know a lot about having to fight things for a good cause, that's why we love playing *Zelda*. It's also why a boy slapped me when I kicked him under a picnic table in Jubilee Park for looking up Cemile's skirt.

You'd think that would have stopped me looking out for her. She wasn't grateful and just kept staring

in shock
at my own shock.

crossed a line, another line.
do it again, always do it again.

run out of whys
just splash water on my face.

such a stress, she's such a stress
funny how all I feel is bliss.

AYLA: NEUTRAL

When I see him this time with our children around him, I know I'm here for the kids. I sit back for them to see him and feel happy because they get the best of him. I recognise the best of him without the familiar belly drop and for the first time I am zooming out, looking at him with all the neutrality I used to wish for when I was pregnant and Anne was pointing at my belly, big again, telling me how she didn't get why I did this. If he came to my door now, I wouldn't close it but I know that I would open it as a friend.

It's all done now. What money I made with Topuz Paşa goes towards the debt the kid's dad had us in with Babo's lot. Nehir supermarket and its merry band of racketeers has been palmed off to a family man who can handle his own. Now I walk past it and feel no claim. All this time, this man in here could only make calls for me, and calls I had already made ... He passes his fingers over his lips as he looks at me over Erhan, İpek and Damla. There is a spot on his neck that he's scratched to almost seem a love bite. The mother in me wants to anoint him with kolonya, the same way I'd douse myself in it as a child to ward off mosquitoes. My perfume from the front door spritz goes to his nose and he can smell that I am older. We speak about Ufuk and his daughter Filiz, how she robbed him after his last deal and took off with Arjîn. How Babo got his ones to find them as a cross-party favour for Yusuf abi, making waves on the scene for diplomatic efforts in the Green Lanes vicinity.

Kids' dad is visibly in the story with me, hands gripping his plastic chair. I'm not sure if he's concerned for Filiz (who babysits for us sometimes), or angry for Ufuk. Although they are not friends, men like this get angry for men like that. He should be angry for me. Arj has embarrassed me. Filiz used to come to the park by my home and see him all the time. Turning a blind eye is what it's called in England; in my home, Anne would tell me not to think too much about other people's problems.

Damla observes me from her chair and her ears could be pointy from how she is straining to hear me. Giving up, she puts her fingers to her dad's teeth. A game. He'll be out soon and will need to make a home but first he'll have to go far. Only distance will free him from the claim his former career has on him. Hands on his trouser waist, he still carries himself like a suited charmer. Prison has stopped his rush, his need to slip away and sleep off heroin. It's left behind medicine, and a weariness that eats his fatherhood. Erhan and İpek argue beside us over who gets which chair. They end up arguing over space, claiming the moon for themselves and refusing to share it.

We all look up towards the ceiling at the LED overheads and spend the final minute of our visiting time imagining we're already outside, looking at the sky.

BABO: BRICKS

This business of mine has small tweaks here and there, but overall what I need to be the same is the same. I swap people's faces out. Arjîn made his bed with the Cypo's daughter, they made a kid and then police got him. He has a limp from what her dad did to him, even though the rumours pin that limp on me. I don't care so much because he knows why he got beats. But over the years, business changes. The most prosperous time in my life is gently coming to a pause. We argue over smaller amounts and I can feel my bird collection is really picking up. I watch the birds with my cat, and we both prick our ears up when the feathers in their chests rustle. If the door bangs outside, it's inconvenience now because me and the animals are all disturbed at once.

I think about Yusuf, men like that who never seemed so flash. Some are retired with their fingers in casino pots, their back and sides covered by government types. Nothing has gone wrong with me except that I've planted too many weeds and now they curl away from me. I haven't the energy to nip things in the bud, and here I am reminding myself of my mother. Her long face always so weathered, nothing hurt her fingers and she never hugged much. All her stories of greed ... She tells me new ones from her head, about the man who hid his gold in mud and straw bricks, thinking that nobody knew. Feeling his death draw near, he returned to his bricks — breaking each one to extract his gold as the load-bearing wall in his house tumbled down. With each crack he looked and looked only to see there was no gold, and he realised all his enemies had been replacing his special bricks with the same bricks that had built the entire hamlet around him. He looked to his old wife, his impoverished children and had nothing to give them, having given nothing. Dayê^{Mum} loved this story, and used to tell it to my father so he'd bring her home extra nuts for her halwa, even during the food embargoes. She almost flirted with him like this, hinting that halwa was a fertility food.

Kurmanji

The Londoner boys. They buy a bottle of Grey Goose for every table at a club birthday and think they've proved their weight. My mother's story would be interpreted by them as permission to splash out. They turn up to assessment centres and trip up the stairs; the biggest readers blame illiteracy on their career setbacks and it's a game for some to get sacked at every cover job they have. I'm tired of calling them in. One ran into Nehir supermarket recently and threatened to have the owner's belly on the counter, a cabbie had to come by to stop him. I don't have time for this.

I was a poor child. One day in my youth my cousin comes to me in Mêrdîn with a suitcase full of clothes. Posh woman, one of the first of us in London. She opened it and said, pick what you want, and I didn't like that. I was only maybe sixteen, I didn't like that, I didn't take nothing. I know she wanted to help me but the way she done it . . . these Londoners have a different mind. All right, maybe I needed it, but the way she done it, I didn't want it. Can you imagine at sixteen, you have nothing and still you don't want to take that opportunity? The reason was, where was you all this time when we struggled and why didn't you come to help my mum? When you grow up you can look after yourself, they were too late. My life was happy until this time to have cushions and a TV that's it, what do I need from these people that I can't get myself? She come back to take me to London and I went with her but I didn't take her clothes. I've actually been putting my own stamp on London, the other day I even took in a cockatiel that I saw flying around Ally Pally. It's such a happy bird but I do wish it would stop waking me up by making a police siren in its mouth.

AYLA, LOOKING AFTER MAKBULE, 2001

Learning what irony means in adulthood is a great way to be chastised by Allah. I spent so long fantasising about cabbages with Topuz Paşa. Now it's a year on and I'm learning about cabbage atrophy as Anne's brain shrinks. The joke is not lost on me. I've done a speck of evil and so I see it. Me or one of the kids give her a spoonful of Marmite every morning. It does seem that the electrical activity in her brain has increased with the Marmite. This morning she takes a spoon and then smacks her lips at me and shakes her head. I ask her what she's thinking.

—Nothing, annem, ^{my child} when I get better, I will think again.

The Turkish woman from the cafe with the blotchy arms, who likes Anne, comes and tells me that I'm getting it wrong. The NHS will tell you anything. They even tell you not to give Marmite to someone with dementia, and that you must only use their prescribed medicines. I am using both, double-timing the medicine with the Marmite. Zade read that you can use peanut butter instead although it doesn't stimulate electrical activity to the same extent. In my village in Kıbrıs, when some of the old ones reach a point where their minds are failing, everyone calls them 'bunamış', thinking them foolish-minded old people. They would say this while simultaneously giving them walnut jam or tahın, to help wake their brains back up. Cafe Woman thinks it's funny to call Anne bunamış.

Anne is sleeping but it is as though her eyes see through the lids. From her Freedom bed with its levers and pulleys, her illness has an active presence and makes the whole room feel surveyed. The NHS didn't tell me about the bedsores she would get from inactivity. I have to monitor my reaction when I lean down to clean them just in case her eyes shoot open when the pain gets to her. She mustn't see me worried. The painkillers have opioids in them so I have to be careful about how much I give her. Even the creams are addictive, I'm sure. I put cream on the open cracking skin and try to keep turning her. It's like she's on a hotplate – if I leave her for too long on one side she gets bruised skin, skin that starts to crack. Where I'm not creaming her, I use a barrier-film spray and she spits 'offfff' when the spray stings.

I feel myself becoming another kind of person. Now I'm the one with the scientific mind; before, it was Anne. I think about her in the garden back home, splicing wild mustard with German cabbage to make good Turkish soft cabbage for good Turkish soft sarma. There's something called longitudinal atrophy, doctor man says. If your PTSD symptoms increase over time then that will accelerate the atrophy too. I know Anne is considered a PTSD + patient. The minute that I mention her history, the war and how Baba died, we get served with more reasons why it makes sense that her brain is shrinking. It's a type of deformation. The most harmful aspect of cabbage atrophy caused by PTSD is that the brainstem takes a sharp decline, while at the same time facial recognition and

185

memory are failing. Still, she's hardly a dotard. The tissue loss that doctor man is telling me about is so high, this is in contrast with the energy she still has to talk. It mainly feels as though she is stuck on the same page: in 1974, in the place where she found her husband's head shot to pieces, by a series of caves made to camouflage shooting men. When she took that journey towards Dipkarpaz in a three-wheeled tractor, she wasn't expecting to be one of the only women from her village to find her man.

—He looked like fasulye. *stewed beans* Even his head.

—Who?

—Your father.

Turkish Cypriot —Benim babam? *My dad*

—Evet, *Yes* like overboiled fasulye.

—Beans? I wish you'd kept that one to yourself.

Baba was a good man. But he had a tendency to put himself in unmanageable situations. I wish he'd helped us more in the garden before we left Limassol. Our London house feels like the only thing that was ever ours. Leaving our home in Limassol behind for a house on the north side in Omorfo felt sad. There were orange trees, streets and streets of them. Now it is called Güzelyurt. Baba would have loved those orange trees, more than he ever loved our cabbages.

—Fasulye! That's how I remember him, when I buried him, that coffin going into the ground felt like the tencere *pot* that had cooked him into that mush, at this stage you'd need to put him into a clay pot or a copper pan, that would be better, I think. Not a coffin. I don't know exactly how they got him like that. I told him, don't go out there, don't get involved; leave the island if you have to. And now what have we got? Nothing but beans when I used to have a husband.

She continues in this way until she reaches my love life, which I know is a bit of a joke. It seems like a long time since she's been happy about the kids' father. I'm just so happy that I got to have children by him. I thought that was enough.

—Anne, I chose him, warts and all. He's not a cruel man.

—I don't understand how you let that esrarcı into your life. One person's drug addict is another person's life partner. If I see my man skinny, I feed him instead of judging him. My mum makes me put my hands in my hair.

—Allah knows, maybe I am the one that can look out for him and no one else can. I am capable of a lot more than you think. People like you see a woman with a baby daddy and think that we have no ideas.

—That's what women like you tell themselves when all they've got to show for their twenties are stretchmarks and knock knock teeth.

—Hic dokunmadı bana, not once, you should be at his feet for how he is with me.

—When he's out of prison don't let him put more babies in you. You don't have to take this on, what's the point of everything if this is what we've come to?

—Here's the point . . .

My arm gestures towards the living room door, rotating back like a turnstile. Damla is standing there.

—Come in, Damla, I can see you at the door, annem. Anne, I promise you, no more babies for me. I'm a business brain now. I need to focus on that.

Our talking has made the time slip away, and now Anne's

187

due for her Hirudoid cream again. Yellow skin and varicose veins. Anne's legs look like this after all that time spent in the waterlogged melon fields. But she has other health problems kicking off too. On the phone to the doctors the other day, they ask me to tell her to cut back a bit on the drink. What drink? They've recommended pads for her to wear; large ones that make her underwear feel tight. It is only during her illness that I learn she has stretch marks all over her stomach from the six children she gave birth to, from memories made for each one of us, before she buried five. She told me that she would feed cabbage to her ewes so their pregnancies would go full term. Even though cabbages prolong ewe pregnancies, she learned that cabbage could cause the pituitary glands of an ewe's foetus to atrophy so they're born _Turkish_ slow. I find this out when I try to give her lahana çorba. _cabbage soup_ She is scared of what the cabbage will do to her head. She is calling me fasulye now: I look like I belong in a pot, not in a coffin. She can see me through the shroud.

That evening Anne dreamt she was a child, one of five sleeping in bed with a young husband who couldn't speak. His agitation was what woke them. His face had split into two and his legs were shaking under the covers. She watched him as he tried to push the parts back together before dying with his brain exposed, leaking blood across their pillows. Jumping from the bed, she tried to call for help but was too small to reach the telephone mounted on the wall. She climbed upon the backs of her dead children, reaching and finally grasping the phone before electric hands emerged, mottled by light from the phone, and grabbed her back. Her body pushing through the telephone line, she was taken on a journey through its cosmic signals, hearing a thousand similar calls for help and an operator advising her to remain calm. She woke pressing the two sides of her face together. I found her like this, and rubbed her temples until her eyes started to close and we spoke, my mother resting against my arms.

—I'm dying, annem, just put me in the garden so it comes quicker.

—You're not some dirty pot in the garden. You're not dying. What about the little ones? They need their nene.

As she aged, she shrank down in size to a height that was magically different; feet out like for a plié but pigeon-chested, without the clarity of collarbone that she used to have and enjoy. I pile her hair up for her, a chignon from the turn of the century before, part matted by the Vaseline that I thumb along her scalp line to help with dandruff and the like. It should have been outrageous to her that she was slathered in Vaseline, but I think it brought back girlhood memories of her hair soaked in olive oil and wrapped. Hair shining and thick like a belly dancer.

—Hair shining and thick like a belly dancer until pulled by my hair out of a cupboard.

That is the thing with forgotten memories, your mind is rarely good at choosing what to recall. Her husband, my baba, seems ever closer. She tries to cover herself more.

—It's exactly things like this. I told you to stop whistling at night, the cinler are going to hear you!

creatures in early pre-Islamic Arabian and later Islamic mythology. Not inherently malevolent but in this context 'the minions of the devil'

—I wasn't whistling . . . We're going to get you a hearing test. Don't worry.

—Annem, the longer I live, the more I forget your dad. I remember more about how lahana feels on my fingers than his face.

—Us living good is the best way to remember him, Anne.

—No. It's like he's a leaf that a snail has got to. I can look at pictures but that don't help if I can't remember his smell. The only memory I've got properly is of his death. I didn't even see it.   *This too shall pass, Mum*

—Bunlar da geçer, Anne. Don't think too much, you know what I've told you about thinking too much.

MAKBULE IN BED, SPRING 2001

Ayla doesn't listen to me when I tell her to turn the radio down. Who wants all of these voices? One of them is the man from my dream. Terbiyesiz. *rude, with no manners* I ask him to come and sit at my bed, we have some things to say.

He used to only hear me once I had myself inside out. Robbing dinner too early from the pan, he smacked my bum as if I was a horse.

Sitting on the end of my bed, he reminds me how I made his food spicy on purpose because his doctor told me I needed to cook with less chilli. My cooking would blow his head off. Not the best words, I think. Anyway, it's all fun. Come now, doesn't every wife do what they can to get their joy back? He took it off me after all.

He tells me he didn't take anything. Laughs. Remember the time he took me out of the sink cupboard? Wardrobe, no? Tut. No, sink cupboard. That was silly because obviously the first place someone is going to look is in the cupboard.

The wedding day, when I hid in the cupboard in my wedding dress. It was like he was undressing the cupboard, pulling off the socks at the feet of the cabinet before taking my arms.

The last thing to come out of the wardrobe was my body.

Turkish Cypriot Çekemem o gazık sessini! *I can't take that hustler voice of yours! (Literally: tent pitch voice)*

Turkish Cypriot On my bed, I am closest to my memories of him. More talk, to when he came home to sleep for öğlen sefası. *siesta* His hand fell over the couch and that big rat came past and nipped at his finger. His scream! Heard him and I ran from the toilet (didn't even wash my hands!), I ran straight to his scream and scared that rat off. I took my slipper off and I threw it. The rat was long as a snake and it 'zhuumd' under the couch before disappearing with two of its sisters. The little bitches. So that scream was funny then.

Now I hear the same scream, but it's like it's been put through a butter churn and it comes out same but different. Since he was gone too long, I hear the scream in my dreams and in my daytime. Try to find it. I want to get to the bottom of the scream but it's stuck somewhere. My husband is sad to hear this but he is proud of our daughter.

I used to think that if I felt like I was at the making of a child every time I went to bed then at least there was something namus *honourable* about feeling like a child under him. Now I have only one, and she is a miracle.

Ayla would read these poems to me until I shouted at her to stop with the poems, nobody needs to chuck salt on the slugs. These propaganda things get in my head more than a molla. *an educated religious man. Used in this way she means one who drops by people's houses, bending their ear* She read me a poem about a girl asking her mum for more brothers and sisters so that war doesn't kill them all. That bit of the poem she read fast past, but she made it too obvious and her tongue wobbled so I heard it even more than the rest of it.

He always made me feel so evil, as if I am a fat cabbage, closing up and rotting inside. Capala te filislensin! *Plough the patch until it is ready to grow!* *Turkish Cypriot*
So he kept coming to me.

Little Damla is here now with Erhan. They scare him away. Damla bullies her brother. Makes him pinch my feet so he gets told off and then she comes to sit with me.

We drink together. The zivania is cinnamon-coloured and it makes my head spin. Husband has dropped a verigo grape into the glass. He came in tired today, crashing through the house, danga di dunga. Have you heard the joke? I ask him what joke. About why we call this grape verigo? When the English set up on the island they ate up all our grapes and turned to their hosts to say it was very good, very good.

Behind husband, I use a long spatula to slide dough into our beehive oven. Last week, we tried to make fırın kebap *oven-roasted meat and potato* *Turkish Cypriot* in it, and husband dropped the clay pot inside the oven so we had to eat the meat çıtır çıtır, *crackle crackle* spitting bits of clay out onto the plate. When I go to take the bread out of the oven, husband tips his glass trying to fish the grape out from it. The only thing that eases my mind is little Erhan coming to my bed and pinching my feet. I wish I'd got to eat the bread again.

DAMLA, 2008–2009, SUMMARISED WITH NO OMISSIONS, NONE WHATSOEVER

William had found a new home in a hostel on Vartry Road, in a thatched building that looked almost like a vicarage. He began his days by emerging from his room into a complex made of narrow corridors and oblong doors. We would meet in the hostel's communal gardens, where other visitors would arrive with children or friends. Three days a week I would turn up, clean the room and listen to him enthuse about the skills training he was being offered. He didn't miss anything, from the IT workshops at Wood Green library to free online courses where he started learning to code. William's friends had cleared off at the two-month mark of him moving into the hostel. No couches or lifts to the jobcentre, they just opted out as soon as he was living the wrong adulthood.

Sandra died in her sleep, arm slung over the pull-out how I always remember her. So we kept remembering. On the last day of her nine night, every mirror covered, numbers were small. We stood by a little counter of dishes, corn soup and cassava bread – the works, provisions hot on mouth roof, how only hard food can settle. Dancing for joy and life, for

Sandra. William asking distant relatives to stop putting music on. Toasts to versions of his mum he didn't know. Hugging, holding. An aunt he'd never seen come around during his mum's life turned up. Said he was welcome to move with her to Norfolk, a good life there, and she could get him driving lessons. Told him stories about his mum to soften that out. The more she spoke, the more he resented her memories. He didn't take her offer to move in. Down to a single-tenant occupancy in a property claiming for two, he lost his house and was put straight into emergency accommodation. After a discretionary grief period.

The feeling of his mum's absence stretched on and became us – mainly through my cooking. Every pan was haunted by her recipes. Every movement of mine a kind of possession. He hung by me in my kitchen looking at me cook, watching me move the spoon like his mother. What began as a flattering request for certain dishes became a needling routine.

We tried to talk it out. Ease the missing with his own memories. He ironed out all his references to her, prefacing them with the words, 'God rest the dead in the living and the looking.' I copied him, trying not to let the words divorce from their meaning while at the same time lost in the idea that the restlessly dead are looking at us through mirrors. He spoke, too, about the dead looking back at him. He became increasingly aware of his reflection. Our relationship moved into another phase, where he did solidly good things and I did good things back.

Sometimes when he came to me he would stop to get food for us, treat day for İpek and Erhan. There was a place near Seven Sisters Road that did the best lahmacun for £1. He'd get it with burger sauce and red cabbage, then turn up at my door with a small crate of it. My mum was always too busy to meet him, but my siblings loved him. He complained about the skunk breeders who lived opposite me. One of them went to school with us. This was a guy who had no game about him, but was particularly enthusiastic about his recent Strawberry Banana Sour strain that he described as a heavy hitter. I don't think anyone wanted a heavy hitter. I would tell William these stories, or about the time I got hit in the face with a pipe. I pointed out the telephone boxes outside my house where police would tap into conversations coming from the farm. I would tell him with glee, like it was something out of the TV, until suddenly I could see that his head had gone and I'd said too much. I wasn't a bespectacled Velma Dinkley, to him I was just a girl with a big mouth. Big mouths don't pay.

After time at mine, he'd smuggle me into his place as if I was a secret. Every time, he apologised for the state of it. I focused on the cracks between the walls and stroked them with my fingers like I could fill them if I had enough intention. It was redolent of both potential and disaster. I thought if the cracks were veins how much those veins would jump at every sensation felt. The room was an abdomen, taking a breath each second. At times like that I would look at the walls, fixing my eyes back on them until the belly of them grew. When we slept together, I couldn't help but think of the oddness of it all, and another friend would flash through my head, prettier than my eyes being open.

William's mother was present in his every movement. He smelt like her too and sometimes when he looked at me I felt her gaze fix upon me. In a way, his body was an empty sack sinking in on itself; every time I tried to prop him back up he would retire into himself. He was never fully present in a conversation when we lay beside one another, with his fingers roaming over my belly.

He was due to start a new job checking people in at Wood Green Civic Centre, reviewing applications and answering complaints. He was told to wear a good clean uniform and it was recommended that he went first to the Matalan beside the shopping centre to find cheap school shirts large enough for an adult. Once he got money in, he had a month to get it all together and find a new place. He found one quickly, something neat and small near the farm. Later, when he returned home from work, his breast pocket would be stuffed with little pens that he collected throughout the day and gently placed on the kitchen counter every evening. They would roll off and slide under the fridge, along with warm used-to-be-frozen peas and paperwork.

On his way to work one day he missed his connecting bus. The closest he got was the bus stop signs flickering by the side of his eye – The Swan pub – Bruce Grove Station – Ponders End – each stop blurring together while the same image stayed fixed in his mind, so clearly that it was like it was pinned to his forehead. His girlfriend in her garden, smacked with a soup spoon. When someone asked the driver where they were, he realised he had ended up in Freezy Water. An old couple near him were sharing Bakewell tarts: nice, boring. He watched them putting their Tupperware away before the last stop.

Some people have songs stuck in their heads all day but he had sound bites stuck in there instead, playing over and over again. Extracts from a conversation. A game show buzzer. A policeman's boots. The sound of rain clattering on your roof. I had brought something into his life. As much as I was body-body and comfort in his life, as much as I missed his mum with him, I was also stress.

He took to reading about himself, trying to get into the heart of internet folklore for his roots. I get to his one day and there's a pair of clogs outside the door. I come in and he tells me jumbees don't have feet and would spend the whole night trying to get the shoes on, shoving into the shoe before moving onto you. I ask him where in hell did he find clogs? The next night I stop off at Wood Green market and get five pairs of pumps for £12, I line them up by the door. We come out the next morning and three pairs have been stolen, another bashed in by the elements, one pair with bird poo in it and the clogs in perfect order. He tells me my shoes are bad luck and throws them onto the street, then asks me to leave the house.

I spent that day in the doghouse burning CDs for him and when I arrived with a small flick case full of them he played through them at his computer. Each time he felt the joy of a song buoyant in his chest, his mood would sink faster at the thought of all that happiness in the world that he wasn't part of. A brief flash of interest before his mood washed back in. He was a dedicated computer man by this point. Username owtflut. He was obsessed with watching videos of beach parties on Reddit and seeing people jump into the cool water. It was like he was trapped under the skin of yoghurt and wanted to push at the skin from beneath to get that same fresh air. Every time he activated the fantasy of blogger girls posing by infinity pools they were more 3D than me. I was a bit of curdle you get stuck in. I was every grimace when he forced himself to drink ayran with our kebap. Stress. That cellulite-y tang that didn't fit with what he wanted. Too much past uncomfortable. When we broke up, I missed the normal of him and how normal he made me.

> I'm gone-off cream.
> Floating to the top of bashed-in plastic.
> Pressed up against the lid.
> I knock into the sides of the tub.
> Plastic on bone.
> I leak out all over his hands.
> His hands, covered in paper cuts.
> I think I am yogh to him, but I am lemon on the sore.

It was the next guy's job to hop on and off trains all day, picking up loose rubbish. He wore a high-vis jacket that said TRAIN PRESENTATION and smiled a lot. Recently I'd been feeling vertigo – also known as a desire to fly – so I was relieved when the train pulled up so I didn't jump over the yellow line. He comes up to me one day and says he saw me looking at the tracks. The next day he sees me and says he saw me bunking the train. I tell him I'm only going one stop. Where do I go for one stop every week? He has started to work out that I am going to the jobcentre. He said, you once threw away an application for a retail assistant job. Was I doing it to catch his attention, the throwing away? Another time, he saw me unwrapping Falım, took the wrapper from my hand before I had the chance to read my fortune inside it. It tastes so bland, how can you eat that? That's the point of this gum, you chase the flavour. It tastes of nothing. The wrapper gets chucked in the bin.

This guy never cares to step foot in my house. He tells me to meet him at his instead, and eventually I do. He shares a permanent council house with his brother by Silver Street station. These houses are part of a square, with wheelie bins in the middle for residents to carry their waste over to. When I get to his door, he holds a pinkie-sized glass, makes a joke about his virility and drinking Magnum. He has draped a checked white bandana around his neck, which he's matched with a monochrome Ecko zipper jacket. Hanging by the door is a NY Yankees cap, which covers a hook where he hangs his keys.

This guy seems a real one. We bond over mapping out the entirety of North London while we chat. You know Broadwater Road? I grew up right there! Everyone is his cousin. He tells me about ringing up the round-the-clock customer line for Eros nightclub all the time asking about their dress code and the little ways in and out of it. He still to this day remembers the last four digits, 'seveny thiveeee sssixie thiveeee'. His barber messed up the slit on his eyebrow on one of his big clubbing days in Enfield – instead of a diagonal one at the end his eyebrow was split in half by a horizontal line, which made him look as though someone had rubbed him out. On his first night at Eros, he tells me about the Avirex jumper he wore with the letters rex standing out bigger than the rest. He wore five rings, two of which he's sure he lost on the night. They were beautiful and white gold, he tells me. One from the pawnshop, one from his mum (which looked just as nice on a man's hand) and the rest from Argos. The only ones he has left now are the Argos ones and that's actually really annoying because they were the cheapest-looking ones. It is nice to be with someone who talks so much. When I go to leave, he gets really pupilly-eyed and heavy on the pulling. I suggest a McFlurry, which puts some time in between us.

Over the ice cream, I tell him about the things I can make. Name enough dishes to get his mind whirring. Is this you saying a McFlurry isn't good enough for you? Are you talking about baklava because you don't like English things? What begins as him being impressed by the range of food I can cook starts to bother him. He hates spicy food. He thinks about each culinary checkpoint of mine as a guy's family that I've learnt the food from. Too much travelling about and eating at everyone's kitchen like some kind of rat.

The first night, he told me I was different from other Turkish girls and I told him that I was Turkish Cypriot. His laughter after that irked me but still his hands got my chin tipping up, softly craning. It felt like a formulaic repetition of whatever had worked in his life leading up to this point, and some of the repetitions worked. Anyone can give pleasure, those algorithms tweaked to a bodily advantage. He told me I was the best and I collected the title, resting on the ghosts of his past lovers, counting each stroke of mine as one to be compared. He played Maxwell and the way he sang along annoyed me. I wondered if he could even understand the lyrics. These songs were written to show the shortcomings in men like him. Anyone in my family would call a man like him dry. Dry men don't leave, though.

He seems to have a harmless clinginess about him. Some sort of appreciation for me speaking to him, I think. He likes things very simple. Has a collection of functional swords. To my disappointment they are mainly European medieval swords. There's no Vlad the Impaler-style sabre. None like the curvy ones out of *Aladdin*. Most of his collection are essentially wall hangers and the only one that looks ready for hitting out with is a bog-standard rapier. All of his wages go on this. His mum buys him swords too. She's moved in with her boyfriend abroad but brings back whatever she can stuff in her suitcase. When I give them a light cleaning and dusting with some cloth and vinegar, he doesn't want me near him for days. It's almost funny. I return after a week and he's lined up the rapiers, Viking-style swords, arming swords and long swords inside a locked cabinet that takes up his entire bedroom.

Over the eight months we went out, we moved the position of our bed four times. Each move spelt a different mood in our relationship. We were at our best in front of the window, when our worst argument was me waking up to see he'd ordered an Albion sword for £800. Soon everything I did wound him up, even in the middle of the night. When I wake up and try to share my nightmares with him before I forget them, he stares at me with disgust on his face, waiting for me to say something worthwhile.

My friend Angela has got me a part-time job in the travel agency she has opened with her mum. Majestic Air Tours. I work as an administration assistant, filing for them, processing visas and checking reservations are made. Angela is still a campaigning woman. She has designed a few types of travel packs for trips to Ghana. One is a five-stop educational tour, beginning with a guided stop-off at a game reserve to get up on a tree platform and watch birds, ending with a trip as far north as Mole National Park. You pay a little bit more for the Romance package. The other is a straightforward trip to Accra, with luggage transfer and a car rental. I often wonder if the Romance package is romantic, and contemplate quizzing the few couples that go.

I'm sleeping best with this nine to five. When it gets to ten, I can just tap out of being awake with no repercussions. Sleep is a healthy thing again, justified because I need to go to work in the morning anyway. I don't get up with that feeling like I've had someone walking around me for ages before they had to leave the house. I'm up first. I love being up first and the feeling of closing the door so I don't wake my mum. I wake up and it's like an intracranial pressure is being syringed out. Oxygen sluicing back in. There's actually a day to start.

The only thing is, what if I was with William instead? Maybe we'd prop each other up. We'd be mutual in not wasting those pennies. His mum would have been happy to see us put our coin to scaling up. Maybe buying something. Or going to one of the places I sell to customers. He always wanted to go to see the mangroves on the Essequibo islands, saying their roots were like ghost fingers. We would have the money to invite friends over, and if he got stressed I'd be able to come back with something in my hands to cheer him up. With this money all I want to do is fix things. I start feeling like I'm in a game of Supermarket Sweep, stockpile cupboard treats and toilet paper. Triple Velvet with its 'three tree promise' so I know what I buy is getting planted back into the ground. There's a Swedish forest somewhere with my name on it. Topuz Paşa is always telling me how you actually make steadier income working in McDonald's than doing what he does. At McDonald's there's nobody to split profit with and when you're at the burger-flipping part of your career ladder, you're one of many colleagues living at home with your mum and working another job to get by. My deal with Angela is good though, I've traded in some of my hours and in exchange I get money. That's more than what you'd get doing smaller run-around jobs.

When I lose the job eventually, Angela tells me it's only because they don't need anyone. If they did, they would have me. It's all part of a rebranding. She plans to start working with Study Abroad agencies. Her role is changing, and we all need to adapt because of this recession. She's refining her offering to include liaison with students from the University of London and writing market intelligence reports to send to partner universities. Nobody said 2009 was going to be an easy year. It's all very complicated. At the jobcentre, I sign on, but the waiting stretches too long.

This guy that I am starting to call my boyfriend reminds me that what we work for is rarely what we achieve.

He then recommends a job with TFL, the union is the best out there, you can't go wrong with RMT.

He comes into the room and finds me pouring water from one glass into another. It's been keeping me alert, making sure not to spill a drop.

The sound of the water sloshing makes me feel I have my ear to the garden, an early-morning ear, just as my mum chucks bleach water out onto the concrete. I used to watch the lines of water connect with one another, running off the surface towards me and taking out ants on the way. A swimming lesson in action, the ants would curl into balls until they pittered off at a ridge in the floor, unfurling legs quickly to climb up and away. Some of the ants couldn't survive the chemicals.

The glass is smacked out of my hand and I am on my back. Man on me like weight. Everything feels fine except for my forearms, which don't like being pressed down.

The water dries on my arms under his hands. I think a lot about his hipbones. They clack when they hit mine. Fingers of sunlight flow along my skin and I look at the shapes they cast, thinking how the more the light distorts my skin the more each cell will coruscate. The high vis is gone. I can hear the ghost of a train that rumbled past a minute ago. A blanket has been chucked over me but the floor wakes me up with its coldness.

I go home to my own bed. İpek is fourteen today. She's asked not to have a big party, so we light the coals and chuck meat on. Topuz Paşa has walked in with hot pide from Green Lanes, he tears it and squeezes the bread down onto the meat, soaking it with the juices. Panny brought the beef sausage in his coat and can't see that the pastırma is covered in fluff from his pocket. When he adds it to the grill, we look suspiciously at it until the fibres have burnt off. I focus my knife on dicing tomato finely to put with çoban salatası, the shepherd-ness of the salad coming from the offloading of leftover long green peppers into the serving bowl. My family talk to me while I chop, each slice hollow on the chopping board. They become heads bobbing in front of me saying things that I need to find the appropriate answer to. Some energy here, in not showing feeling on my face.

a glass flies through air

forearms not flying with it
    can't cover my face
    clack
    go with the hipbones so I can sleep

·

When I go back to his to pack my bags, he comes to talk to me. It occurs to me that none of this stuff was really worth coming back for anyway.

—But you know I love you.

After a few repetitions of 'I'm not convinced' and 'I can't be forgiving that', his face switches.

That face again.

The same face as the man with a tent to show me.

Look, it's a tepee.

He comes towards me and I hit out with his work boot. A steel toecap flies straight towards his head and he's out. His face looks as slack as someone who belongs transcended on a soiled Anatolian rug. I smash the cabinet in his bedroom and remove the swords. I carry them out and leave them by the front door one by one. On the floor, the swords are a fallen fence.

That night, I tell my mum. How he was awful, maybe out of character.

—Awful and out of character can happen again.

She told me to look at the men who break women's spirits. To look at their skin. The sheen of sweat climbing their throats. The flushed skin. The way their smiles curdled into impish stretches of lip and rotting teeth. See how their hair has started to recede and fall out. He looks unhappy, doesn't he?

—Men who break a good woman start to rot from the inside, out.

•

The next day, I'm sitting in a car with Topuz Paşa and ex comes towards us and raps on the glass. His tap has a folksy urgency to it, the second and third taps closely following one another. He has a brindle eye from the soaring boot. Topuz Paşa looks at me and starts humming. He carries a lot of his age inside his moustache but above it he has the type of aquiline nose that makes a person's eyes look merrier, and merry here translates as young.

—Creepy git, isn't he?

He rolls the window down, tells him to hop in and me to hop out. By the time I'm out of the car, they're both driving off fast as. I sit on the brick partition opposite my house and wait for about half an hour. When Topuz Paşa returns, there are bits of ripped branded clothes stuffed in his pockets. He gets out his car and shows me a sword. Told me he offered my friend a lift home. Doesn't tell me how he got the sword but I recognise it anyway.

This is a Hersir Viking sword. It's a Type H hilt in Petersen's typology that can be found on swords dated to the period between the second half of the eighth century and the second half of the tenth century. An absolute classic, it doesn't feel cramped in your hands at all. A limited edition of only five hundred collectible swords worldwide. The only shame is that the hilt has not been damascened with wire inlays of copper alloys, tin and silver. I can't wait to leave it out in the rain.

DAMLA, AT HOME, 2011

We circle over the same territory. It makes you notice the chip on a surface that you nearly missed. A mark in a carpet from a tooth bucked into it by one flying mother, both a ridge in the fabric and a stain. My mum has her little tooth trapped in the wood of our house. Burgling men tooth. She put her tooth in a jar and never put anything else back in her mouth. By the time İpek has found her earring, our fingers have brushed over enough textures. Just because life has moved on, we still feast with memory, collect and wipe its crumbs from our lips. We are told that cinler are a pestilence of demons, they catch you while you are glancing in the mirror and fix your eyes. But I believe that there is no catching; only meeting and staying. This troupe of cin have followed me for so long now that I recognise their footsteps. Even as an adult, I know them. I know them by the tremor in my hands while I make love, that fear which swaps out one person's face for that face, that man. Maybe this is what makes my mind go to Cemile, awake or asleep in bed I think of her and it's like water, so calm. I always slept easiest beside her, though.

I speak with İpek about this because she makes me feel taller than the ceiling, curled down with our foreheads touching.

She knows. I follow her in and out of the kitchen while we speak so she can get us spoons.

İpek is proud of our brother, who wants to do BTEC Business. He plans to put the family somewhere legit and doesn't like how everybody on benefits is scared to show themselves. I don't know how this works around his girlfriend at Nehir supermarket, maybe he's going to offer to do their books when he's not in school. As it stands he's just like security, pole-straight by her while she works the till and admiring every time she holds a heavy box before remembering to help her hold it.

I'm eating bio-yoghurt and as I smooth the spoon over the top of it, I unearth the little bits of strawberry and they resemble old blood clots. Probably the closest thing that I've seen to compare them to, unless we're talking end of day at the halal butchers – when there's only the raggedy meat, chilling in the polystyrene, flies chilling too. Reminds me of Cemile's stories about faking your virginity; I bet she'd never have considered strawberry bits from yoghurt. The fabric under our sofa has frayed. İpek tells me that's actually called a cambric desk cover. I don't follow up on what she says with a google. Cambric desk cover. I see old desks, and find myself irritated that they do not have this material. If I were to invent desks, I would have my Type 1 desk with a plush underside on the front-facing section of the desk so that the top of my thigh wouldn't touch wood. At the back of the desk, which wouldn't be visible to the lazy eye, there would be a cambric desk cover.

I'm reminded of that bike ride with Cemile that could have gone on forever, if only the sofa hadn't stopped her. So many memories of her have the farm looming over us, I'm sure we'd have got away with more if it hadn't been checking for us.

NEHIR SUPERMARKET, 2011

Erhan goes to the toilet so quick whenever he is at Nehir supermarket because he doesn't want to leave his girlfriend Şilem alone at the till. Her dad used to want her to be a bus driver or a policewoman because of her strength. Şilem once booted down two solid doors to get to her friend who'd tried to drink herself to death inside her mum's house. Fourteen – like Erhan. She's grown.

Despite this, Erhan is still surprised to return from the toilet and find Şilem pinning down a punter in the doorway of Nehir supermarket while simultaneously yanking a four-pack out of his hand. He runs over and tries to help, yelling out for more people to come. They know that he might come back again and don't consider ringing for an ambulance or the police, there are too many people like this to keep track of around here. Sometimes the shopkeepers might be kind and offer a free lollipop to someone who comes in staggering. Most times they are watching the small TV above their heads with one eye, the other waiting to catch their thieves in action. It is becoming clear to Erhan that this is his home, and he feels protected.

DAMLA: THINGS WORK A CERTAIN WAY, 2011

My mum told me how Nene didn't know what green was. She once told me that in her village they used to gather up bushels of it, tuck them all together and sweep the floors with it.

Small-time gangs here sell green like a pressure cooker, running around ticking and hissing to make what others make in one second with brown and white. Arjîn abi used to tell Cemile and me about how people need to upgrade themselves before they have their cars robbed and sold for £200. If you're unlucky you'll get robbed again walking home by NPK yungers.

Cemile and I observed the ones who stepped up – the ones from Hackney doing more than expected. You can sell a bagful of cannabis, or a handful of heroin, and you get more money out of the handful than the bagful (common sense, I know). Erhan gives us information from all the shop talk around Nehir and it is funny how we're watching things change, but from the outside.

Transportation is big money. I know this now. Knowing means that I'm not the woman that sweeps floors with weed brooms and stockpiles cutting agent for a man, thinking that he wants baby formula.

Filiz is that girl. Her mind is all on Arj. Her mind is all on what they smoke too. His arrest changes things in London but it takes us some time to act on the change. There is some worry that Ufuk abi snitched on his own son-in-law out of spite, and that doesn't get ignored by Babo. Ufuk abi is in Kıbrıs.

Anne has become more quiet. Reminiscing about cabbages. She wants to change her brain, closer to her mum, she wants to be in a village sweeping with brooms of weed, head in the dust.

Arj only got fifteen years, but if he is good he can come out on tariff after seven years, so his child is growing up without him in Kıbrıs. He didn't talk. Everybody talks in Turkey but over here it's different. If you get caught in Turkey you've had it. In Turkey they beat you so much you have to . . . there's special rooms in every police station where they make you talk. It's known. Everybody knows if they take you into that room, electric shocks, everything. The Filistin falakası, Palestinian hanging, where they tie you onto the stick and raise you up from the back, and you're up just like that . . . ooh, torture and a half, man. So in Turkey there's no such thing as a grass, everybody talks, according to what Topuz Paşa tells me.

—The funny part is that they put everyone together. Say you got nicked, you're stuck with the eight people out of nine that you grassed on. We're all in one big open prison. All the arguments are 'you gave them up, why you giving us up too?' And then chats. Sometimes getting beaten up. But over here? You'd get sliced up to pieces. They'd never risk putting you in the same prison as someone you grassed on. In English prisons they have this system where, if you have any enemies in there, you're at least really far away, one on one side and one on the other, you would never meet, if you talk and people get to know, you get moved again.

In the old days Turks would be doing so much street dealing but now they're higher up than ever, all the big bosses. Turk babaları. All the chemists are Turks and Kurds. Just because the babas here get caught doesn't mean all your pies aren't stuffed with fingers that are far away. They're being covered because the police are chasing the London kids who think that they're the daddies of one postcode, they play. Don't confuse the ball chasers for the owners of the club. Everything gets done through phones. Topuz Paşa continues:

—I do miss when your passport was clean if you were coming from Romania. All they suspected was Turkey back then. In the nineties, lots of small cars. English families in camper vans filling up on twenty kilos for their transport fee.

—Technology has made them invisible, it's gorgeous. But on the road you need to sell to at least twenty people a day, and each addict will quickly ID their dealer. I wanna know what retirement looks like for these men. If you can make it for one year, you are the luckiest man on earth.

DAMLA: BOWLING
AND RIOTING, 2011

We pay £1 to come in with food and sit with a dürüm each,^{kebab wrap} watching the bowlers. Angela rolls her eyes at Sean Paul getting people running from the bowling alleys to the dance floor, so obvious. I don't roll my eyes cos I think this is the best thing about music: the classics, the cheesiness of it and the way you get time back for yourself when they all leave the floor the minute the real good one comes on.

There's a boy next to us who reminds me of a boy Cemile used to see, and he looks at us while he flicks a lighter. As the wheel gets pulled back it sounds like a toenail clipper. If my mum was here she would probably tell me not to look back, that I'm encouraging him. I know I'm not being heard when I tell her that sometimes people look when you don't look, so you might as well keep your eyes open. Our home is empty of her so often that I have to keep one eye ready to meet whatever's out the window, and one inside on Erhan and İpek.

Angela is doing so good in her new travel agency that she's partnered up with a community garden, sponsoring them to host cooking classes themed around holiday packages that she's put together. I volunteer with the garden during the day. When Angela's classes are scheduled in, she pays me to help her put them on and gets her mum to list me with instructions to farm out to the yuppie couples huddled around the picnic benches that I have dragged together to form a haphazard circle. Today I smell like garlic and crayfish. Angela's mum makes an okra stew with crayfish that reminds me of William and my mum at the same time. Unlike William and my mum, she grinds everything down to almost powder when she makes the base for her stews.

We're doing just fine for two twenty-year-olds, despite everything going on around us.

There's some trouble outside that we're just starting to notice and nobody is wanting to dance, bowl, do anything any more. I get a text saying there's no damage going on outside that should be keeping us inside, so we leave. I'm glad for Angela that she'd wheeled her bike inside, and glad for myself that I don't ride a bike. It's better to walk and have your eyes properly open that way – no wind to make your peripherals blurry. Angela kicks a bin outside the bowling alley, bins are the council's problem so the best thing to kick. It's half seven and a bunch of police run from the station opposite us and fan out trying to block things off into the park. My mum sends a text asking me to go and get a jumbo pack of rice if it's free-for-all tonight. Apparently people are rallying in the car park of the Tesco in South Tottenham, but they're only trying to grab stuff to chuck at the police, not to loot.

We sardine-jump on the train to avoid the streets, and walk back from Turnpike Lane. Angela's phone is with Orange and her network goes down for a bit. She's worried about her dad on trains and hopes he's home already – trains are always impossible when you've got crowds like this. When her service comes back, her mum reassures her that her dad is finishing his shift. On my phone, the mayor is thinking out loud on Twitter about cancelling his holiday early to fly back and sort it out.

On the walk, riot vans rock past. It's near eight. Angela and I are alert, a fresh type of awake, watching our area erupt around us. The trainers on the tree near Bruce Grove are still there – things aren't so big different. We laugh at the stuff coming through on our phones, the quiet villages in the sub-urbs that are apparently more of a riot central than here. So many mad stories too on BBM, the way people are fighting each other for scratch cards in our Ladbrokes. From what we saw, they're not fighting for them and they're being quite fair about it – take a stack and leave a stack for the people behind you, get there early and it's even sweeter. No one is hearing anyone.

Some of the Facebook groups I'm in are putting pictures up of London and it's wild cos these pictures aren't even England, one person posts tanks in Egypt and says that Bank in central is on fire. Can't even get the country right. We laugh more too when the tiger that had left London Zoo to join the riot was actually another fake picture, taken from a tiger who went on a walkabout in Italy in 2008.

And there definitely isn't a mob of two hundred Turks chasing down the police in Dalston. On the phone Topuz Paşa rings to say that on Green Lanes it's mad, boys about there are tanking up with energy drinks. He said he held a door closed when seven men tried to barge into Moruk. When I ask him to repeat himself he says there were actually fifteen men in total but it was seven who were pushing the door while the rest were trying to come round the back. I never know if I should believe him. Mostly Turks and Kurds around the area had formed little pockets of security, doing what police wouldn't.

Anne texts me saying if I'm still walking she can text him to come get me but I know Topuz Paşa's got things to do, and me and Angela are nearly back now. Her little brother Kwame is with Erhan and İpek at mine so she's just going to stay with us until her dad comes for them. You're never too old for a lift from your dad, she says. I can imagine that would be true.

When we get in we think of all the people in their houses with bats and frying pans waiting for trouble. As soon as I come through the door, Erhan darts out to run to his girl-friend at Nehir. He texts to say they're fine and staying open because Şilem's dad has got some friends standing around. Later in the night I hear about Enfield Protection Gang, at least a hundred of them and mostly white, patrolling EN3 to stop anyone thinking about joining in with us lot in Tottenham. An industrial estate goes up on fire. Music types are worrying about lost vinyl and some of them are also worried about small companies going bust. I watch people on TV with outdated announcements until I fall asleep, in my dreams I'm a child watching Anne drawing out the anatomy of a cabbage on big stretches of paper.

You can feel all this safety around you. All the time your protection is only two minutes away but still there are these shadows. Big man making promises. All the hotheads banging pans in the middle of a kitchen. These men chucking your dinner at the floor. Some other man asking where your dad's gone now.

Anne slips into the sitting room, sneaky-like to bring me upstairs and turn off the TV. People are still awake outside. She thinks that now is a good time to tell me that London isn't the place for her any more and that she's going back home. Her home is not my home for the first time and suddenly I'm blaming her for everything, especially for men and for our neighbour. I didn't know I could shout like this. People warn you about shouting like this, you can cross a line if you shout too much. As if her bottom lip is pumping something out of her mouth, Anne watches me in a state of shock but doesn't really understand my problem, as I've had it so easy.

Anne has told me that Topuz Paşa will keep an eye on us, and his wallet will too. She's been paying her flight off slowly for the last ten weeks and it's a one-way to Kıbrıs. She'll pass a message to Cemile for me. She'll send me helim with her cousins when they get back from their holidays, the ones I haven't met. She'll ring me; I have to make sure to ring her. A proper one like me should find it easy to keep the house without her.

AYLA: MAN WITCH, 2011

Damla flips out on me one night. Now I cry when I see children. I'm cotton-mouthed from crying. When I wonder what a mother is, I wonder how to remake a mother out of me. *in this* Damla keeps wandering away from the house and meeting cinler. *context, monsters* I wish I'd told her more about life but I don't know as much as I need to teach, I do warn her about men who try to whittle you down and even though the advice is too late, maybe now I give it for next time. I sleep to find her troubles hiding in my dreams. I know I could have done things differently. Lately it seems that motherhood is a crash course in regret.

You get familiar with regret when you've had a mum like mine. After the war, when we had to plant a garden again, Anne cried. Everything has got its own season, even the wild grass. When she started coming through with the çapa,*hoe* *Turkish Cypriot* I wanted to tell her to leave it a bit, take some time. She cursed herself for wasting time, and took it all out on the garden until her legs got even more veiny and the sun made her dizzy.

I didn't realise one day I would be in my own garden with Zade, planting as much as I could along my fences to block out the world. Zade went through this same thing herself when her sister upset her – she put plants everywhere inside her flat, you can see them trailing out of the windows. This is how we mourn. In the sun of autumn, I look up and the serrations of the vine leaves are becoming more pronounced with age. If you peer through the obvious patches of leaves, there are sections where the leaves are still moist and green. This whole garden of mine was planted with Anne, to bring Kıbrıs to her feet. She would push branches out of the way to get into the belly of the yaprak,^{vine} always showing me the way. I wish I could ask her about Damla, and what she would have said to her.

Our neighbour next door is drinking soup in his garden. A man witch, the smell of the broth carries and to my nose is as if he put his foot in it. Another man that hurt my daughter but too long ago for me to know exactly what to do. This man with his ceramic babies. When I was pregnant for the second time, he bought me a bar of English chocolate so large that I could use it as a lid for my biscuit tin. Old age doesn't treat every man kindly, or won't.

DAMLA, NORTH CYPRUS, 2012, THINKING OF 2007 LONDON

Anne pays most of my flight, the rest comes out of my left-over wages. I don't know if it's my island I'm going back to or Cemile's. Cemile is good at being a building. When I think of her she can be Northolt covered with Charlie spray. I could write Turkish songs talking about her, about how she is every road skip that we've crawled into to find wooden bits to hold onto for the fun of looking trouble. But she isn't London to me any more. Now London has picked up extra traits, me tampering with swords and watching Erhan find his own way into veggie shop life. Can Cemile be Cyprus?

If Cemile is Cyprus, how does my mum fit into that? Does she ring Cemile to ask permission if she can grow a cabbage patch? It is like the Kıbrıs I'll be arriving in will have her sprouting out from all the tilled fields, I'll put peppers out to roast on the roof and come back to find Cemile as the end result.

If I think about it, there are some things about London that are so good, so Cemile, I know she must have those memories too.

She left in 2007 after that night in McDonald's, showing me her nuggets and complaining about Turkish fried chicken. It was such a silly way to end our closeness that I knew I'd see her again. But if I really really think, it wasn't so silly. We used silly to cover up a whole lot of real, even just hearing stories of that bouncer's stomach still makes me touch my own. Before that night though, we had the gig at the community centre, our hands on the floor feeling the bass from the clash inside.

The air has us both a bit blissed out. Everyone here for King Tubby's Sound System, and Tottenham's own Fat Man Sound. The lettering for Tubby's logo looks like it's off the Tekken cover. Cemile's not having any of that. Tells me it's because I'm thinking of the letter T and putting all the Ts together in one place. Some of the sound systems here have been playing for near on forty years. Common knowledge. Some younger people have arrived promising to bring the room's energy up, they flit nervously around the MC. The MC presenting calls himself General T and guarantees selections in a 'roots and culture style'. We don't know what he means, but he seems outside of what everyone else is doing, looking at the music rather than being in it. I think he'd quite like a logo like the Tekken cover himself. It's £10 till 11 p.m., and we haven't paid in but there's a lot of good listening from outside the community centre. They let us in early doors to look at the jewellery and T-shirts, merch filling the space, before gently ushering us back out where we sit talking. We get out a crumbler. Twist. Bud down into small pieces. Cemile chips half a cigarette.

When it's time to get out of the way and go home, Cemile talks me through everything she sees. We watch the van getting loaded back up in an order known only to the boys who come to help out every time, they wheel hand trucks past

with great seriousness (probably alert in case of clumsy girls).
Cemile runs her hands over whatever goes past her and is
surprised that the thick cables from the sound systems are
so sticky, not thinking how they've been dragged across so
many different floors. Everything is getting noticed tonight.
I have been walking this bit since I was small but only now
do I hear that MLK Jr is on the Peace Mural. It took me a
long time to even notice the figure floating in the sky of the
mural. When I did notice it I always thought it was a Disney
character with the way he had these brooding prince brows
and a hand to the chin like someone watching me from a shop
door. MLK is deep in thought.

Another boy has hurt Cemile's heart, and I am heartbroken
with her. She has her arm linked in mine and it feels like I have
to hold her up. I ask her if she's ill or something.

Not ill, but she's so tired she comes to mine again. Anne has
not been liking her staying over recently. She says it brings
Topuz Paşa's back up because it puts Cemile's dad Ufuk in
a bad mood even if he knows where she is when she isn't
in his house. Filiz has caused murders for all her running
about with Arj. Cemile has some weight on her recently and
it makes her sweeter to me as the night gets late. We're spliff
floating. I sidle up close to my bedroom wall to make room for
her in my single, the extra space her belly takes up surprises
us both. Without a second, I put my hand on her belly and
watch her as she watches my hand, my thumb stopping where
her belly hairs are starting to grow back from being shaved,
just under her belly button. Has Cemile known? Above us,
my little sister sleeps. I wonder how obvious I've been. We
sigh. I stroke her hair away from her forehead, this hand

cool on the sweat that has gathered. My other hand moves a little more down and I get a kiss for it, and we're breathing. Another quieter kiss before Cemile shakes her head at me and turns over to sleep.

DAMLA AND İPEK
ARRIVE IN KIBRIS, 2012

Anne's place in Kıbrıs is not an ancestor's house. It's a one-
floor stone building tucked tightly between the multiply
extended houses of the villagers. They'd welcomed her back
by bringing her their favourite crossed tomatoes to plant,
and two days after that Anne visited a friend of Nene's who
had grown the same family of cabbages that her mum had
fed her from growing up. Ahead of her arrival on the island,
they cleared accrued clutter from the garden − building
materials and trays put for stray dogs to eat from. She was
reminded of her parents and didn't slow down with their
recollections in line with her prickling up. London had let
her forget that, out here, not much goes unsaid. Even the
oldest memories still turn out the first impressions your
children give, and so İpek and me came for the first time to
a reception. When my nene had fled from her husband after
her wedding day, the whole village remembers him finding
her under the sink. I know that they still handle Anne with
sympathy, that there had not been enough time or resolution
since the war for grieving over the dead. This communal grief
flickered in conversation, circling around itself, around a
plate of karpuz *watermelon* and helim, cooling them down in the heat,

then later into the evening dropping by to join your table and recollecting again.

If I'd known more than what could be said by phone, I think this island would have got me here faster, I'd have thought of it as less a place only for Cemile and more a place that could have been for us. Even the discomfort of a fan instead of air con in Anne's place would have been all right for Cemile and me. When Cemile would sweat, the majority sweat took place under her knees until only legs up would do. Us in Lorship Rec by the kids' play, her legs up and resting over my knees as she dozed with her hair tangling up in the grass. Me feeling upset and directly aware of the men muttering a response to the audacity of a girl sleeping in public.

Anne has adopted a village cat who is basically a domesticated mountain cat. Hair thick and quick to bite. I practise the heat tolerance of my own knees through the cat, who has climbed ankle up to sleep on me.

We have everyone to meet in this place, a lot of new wives with men in white shorts and good fat hairy bellies who've come here to avoid paying child benefit or to reap the rewards of getting in and getting out. There are the expats in Karmi who sit on flowered balconies reading, who come down the steps towards us from the streets and they remember Anne. Eric especially, the closest friend to my dad. People like Eric hold so many memories and they talk, too, folding skirts and making coffee, pulling out books as reference and evidence.

In the internet cafe, Zade tells us more about Erhan via Warren than we know through Erhan himself. We go to the cafe in place of neighbouring Wi-Fi because limited privacy is better than none. The boys at the cafe are too outraged by their own privacy being invaded to cross over, so we talk to Zade freely. The London that İpek and me left behind was cheap to leave, everyone else staying so they could watch the Olympics down the road on their TVs and phones.

Anne teaches me by living. If Cemile was just a friend like Zade, I would have done the same and kept in touch with her easy-peasy. Her phone would have rung through to her voice, and I could have made a holiday out of her leaving. Exiting the cafe, we walk to the beat of our flip-flops smacking back, and she points things out in this new-home, especially the recreations. Things have been put in the same place and individual preferences have been copied over so specifically that yellow-tipped white flowers still flood out of the house of the lady that Anne had neighboured as a child on the other side. She calls out to us and we go in for another coffee, for fear of being rude.

CEMILE'S DAD, 2012

A lamb gets off the conveyer and comes up to him before nuzzling him like a puppy. He puts it back in line and hopes not to recognise it when he has to dispatch it. In his boredom, he practises blowing bubbles of spit, calculating the different notes of popping and how many double bubbles he can blow. During his second week on the job, he lost three fingers. His pay-off was enough to keep the company of his wife too much, and he slept on the couch during daylight hours so she couldn't have guests come inside for coffee, instead was sequestered to the veranda during the hottest hours. Her cooking took a fall because of this; instead of making meals she needed to check on during the day, she made plain stews and left them on the hob all day while she visited house to house.

The farmers in the village are annoyed by Ufuk's job: he's been dispatching animals being brought into the slaughter-house he works at in Lefkoşa. There is no meat inspectorate here but village-scale kills are kinder. Ufuk's job is time-limited. Dairy farming is another industry you can't work in here; nobody wants a cow with bloated udders and foot problems. Instead you pay visits to your favourite neighbour with your favourite goat, and buy helim from them, or you go to the village shop and get long-life milk from Turkey.

Ufuk is still angry with his daughters, mostly Filiz. Angry with his wife too, a little. He still loves his TV and is frustrated by how the sunlight catches its screen during the day. Sometimes the TV has poor connection and he hits it, forgetting his three fingers. He put Filiz's Arj in hospital for sleeping with his daughter, and then Arj comes out of hospital and goes straight to jail for getting caught driving a truckload of cabbage. Babo's still angry with Ufuk for going after Arj, so now he's here in Kıbrıs, as if that will do anything because Yusuf abi is angry with him too.

GOING VISITING,
TWO DAYS AFTER
ARRIVING IN KIBRIS, 2012

Less than a mile from Karmi, a strip of villas has been built. To the public, one looks like a hotel. It is gated. Security patrols it at all points of the diadem compound. The entrance has gold and white engravings of a seahorse tilting itself left. Inside, Yusuf shuffles in his slippers over to his TV. It is 4 a.m. and he curses at the screen as a disappointed football crowd groans too. A lady in a smart salon tunic disturbs him for his daily massage. With his face down in the hole, he is nearly asleep. Soon, he dozes off for twenty minutes while his masseuse applies ointment to the thin skin of his lower calves. She takes the opportunity to put aloe vera on his metatarsals, where mosquitoes have got him. Returning to the most moley area of his body, flesh is pressed in firmly, her finger's path occasionally circumvented by moles. There is one mole on his back that was lost for many years in fat accrued during his time in London. It reveals itself today easily, so loose it could fall from Yusuf's skin.

Like Babo's, Yusuf's brother is also in jail for stupidity. For stupidity, Yusuf advocates a healthy helping of time and solitude, which prison allows. Yusuf wakes from his shut-eye with a smirk, thinking of their last conversation. The Olympics has brought investors back to London, so his brother recommended he sell off some of his properties. He didn't need that advice. Especially considering his brother's recent failed deal.

Yusuf is waking to the feeling of his intestines being jabbed a little. He had recently joked with someone: 'Barsakların çıksın.' *May your insides fall out* He makes these jokes all the time and likes *Turkish Cypriot* how his jokes have some ground on them. He'd once witnessed a man make a jab so deep with his knife that the intestines fell out. Sometimes his memory adds in a dog, who runs off with part of them. The actual events were that the man with the knife squashed a few with his feet before leaving. Intestine guy had managed to protect some and shove them back in, weeping in the foetal position until a friend dropped him off at the hospital.

The massage finishes as usual with talcum powder on his soles and an offer of aftershave. Yusuf spends the next hour checking in on his businesses. He operates just enough to keep himself active. His son-in-law is a good boy who loves his daughter, and his grandchildren park their bikes in his garden. These are the family years, and yet he still imagines Moruk cafe and his humble audience of opportunity men. The mainlanders in the room had to adjust to him, so they are Cypofied still to this day. It is achievements like this that make him feel patriotic.

Most office days finish with sleep. It will be night, a person might be hungry, and those two things will measure their day. Much to the fortune of Yusuf, he gets to nap after his office time before going out to his garden. It's in his garden where his weight went. Muscly arms from tilling imported red soil from mainland, and a tanned back from topless fig collection. He's chosen to receive his guests, Damla and Ayla, here. Damla never looks him in the eye, almost shy in how she appraises his garden. She's already been walked out through his other garden, a foil used to shake hands with old friends but less personal than this one. Damla mentions the differences and how he only has this one fig tree for such a big property. Some could think she's rude, but Yusuf knows her tune. It's longing. He pulls gently on the branch and takes a fig for her. It is closer to yellow than green. Her mother watches in silence as she squashes the fig open, barely peeling it. Damla's forefinger slips up and touches the milk. She is assured by Yusuf that if she puts her hand in the soil beneath her, the earth will clean the glue off her skin.

Soil crumbles from her fingers.

DAMLA: THE NEXT VISIT, DAY 3 IN KIBRIS

I rang ahead to tell Cemile I'd be seeing her in the morning. Her village is a way from mine. I can't drive and so I'm stuck waiting for a lift. Anne has a neighbour who delivers water to Cemile's village, so we wait until he turns up, a cousin of mine who I've never met also jumping in so we don't do the drive alone.

The truck starts up and just when I thought I'd managed to switch something off, I have this immensity of feeling. I keep it in my imagination. How much she said by simply resting beside me. I imagine us two like spiders weaving a house together, something infinite in our making process. The truck shudders to a stop and the driver jumps down to make his first delivery of the day, pointing to the house on his right – Cemile's house. My cousin helps him bring the water in while I go straight to her house. I walk robot fast to her door before the feelings catch up on me.

Seeing her again is like eating a shadow. Her house stands on stilts, overlooking the entire village. It is a new intimacy, the way she leans against its door frame, the cracks in her hard foot sucking up the dust she kicks up, the straps of her slippers sealing in swollen skin.

We sit on the porch steps in the sun and speak with flying hands. Our legs tan as they hang over the steps. The light bounces off my shoes and makes them look like polished noses. She tells me about her first pregnancy. How she ran over to her father-in-law and kept shouting that her waters had broken. He glared at her beneath his hat, then ran off to grab the toolbox. Gradually he came to the realisation while standing there, muttering to himself: her waters – not her water tank – had broken. She was seventeen by the time the baby came and, even though she'd been found a husband, nobody could say the child looked like him.

She was not always sweet and that's what I loved about her. Honey sting. The hoods of her eyes are very beautiful to me; they sit within their sockets in a peaceful way. They are thin rabbit-skinned things, good for a kiss that'd keep them closed. She flickers her eyes back at me and her stare is so tired that my thoughts shame me. There are certain types of needs that make a repetition of you. I had become one of many because of looking for too long. It was as though I'd done the very thing I hated myself, by taking her moment of introspection and rest, taking that time that she chose not to communicate with me, and still eating from it.

she hung back
a breath of complete isolation
break it like water
eyelids open onto me, my lips too
we know

We walk her garden in short laps. She has this habit of flipping her slipper against her heel. It is distracting. At this early hour, the bins, ransacked overnight by local strays, are still waiting to be collected. If she could walk with me into some quietness that would be good. I could tell her more things. There is a condensation around us, a pilgrim's fog that drops upon us.

Taking my hand, she brings me inside her home, and offers me a glass of lukewarm water from the tank that tastes of chlorine. She gives me sunflower seeds to snack on while she takes trays out, makes clatter. I chew tendrils of maydanoz. Translucence in her stare as she looks at me. _Parsley_

Since having her kids she feels as though her breasts are touching her stomach and tells me I could have been a good auntie to them, if things had been different. Time has become too big for us both. Her breasts do not touch her stomach. The TV goes on and conversation stops, replaced by the shelling of beans. Her giggles. Ten minutes into watching her show, she is laughing in hysterics and I can't follow it. After finishing my third tea, I go. On the way out, I bump into her son, returning home with his grandmother. Her son wears a jumper with Fila Italia scrawled over the front, only the letter F isn't written with a red bar for the top of the letter and a line-art gun shape for the bottom. Instead it is an italicised F. In my head I redesign the jumper.

Cemile is a hairdresser now. Glamorous like I wanted for her. Though her curls have been pressed down with straighteners — far from when we perched on cars, a greasy film running down our sideburns from the rain and Black & White wax.

Later in the evening, I leave Anne's house to walk towards the beach. This journey is mysterious at night. I know that the beach is not far, and if it were daytime I might even be able to see an outline of the sea from here. I can't use the map on my phone because data in North Cyprus is expensive. That's OK because I want to get lost. There are empty buildings everywhere from where developers have come and marked their presence but they're waiting for tax rates to drop and tourism here to improve before they finish their builds. There are people who pass through this area to get to the next neck of their journey, and they don't nod their heads to say hello, they just glare. Wild dogs run past with somewhere urgent that they need to be. My legs have already started itching from walking through the park in the village square; whatever was sprayed on the grass is not meant for living things.

On the outskirts of the village, one house is still very much awake and when I look inside I see the water deliveryman sat in a row of plastic chairs by a long table; he is one of many topless men. It is sweet. They promise each other extra food, one man stopping at each of those in the row to offer them *Turkish* meat from a large metal bowl. Pirzolacık, şeftalicik. *lil lamb, Cypriot* Most of the men are bald with beards and have *lil sausage* towels on their shoulders to soak up their head sweat. Whenever one man stands up to run into the kitchen, the man sat next to him is thrilled to be able to put his arm up on the back of the empty chair.

A guitar and a darbuka make an appearance. All the men sing a song about someone whose lips broke after breaking a promise made to a lover. It's strange to me that there aren't women around because usually there would be, and the women would be dancing, arms in angel formation. A small baby is carried over by a boy who I know to be a cousin's cousin and then one of us appears, a lady shouting out at them from the front room. Cigars are puffed out the side of mouths by each of the men who lean forward to say hello to the baby girl before she is carried back in.

Arguing interrupts the music when pulya is brought to the table. Words start flying out. Cıkartı basımıza fasariya problem problem. *You've put a fussy problem on our heads* Some in the group are *Turkish Cypriot* Londoners who've come to visit their family. Water Tank Man's mum had plucked and pickled at least fifty pulya – small vinegared birds – and specifically put them aside for her children from abroad to take back home. You've got twenty and I've only got ten. Gesturing towards little jars on the long table, some of them lean forward to take their portion. The elder brother of Water Tank Man opens his jar and pulls out a greying small bird, its head flopping to one side, and eats it whole. The next one he pulls out looks like a blackcap. His mum puts a bowl down for people to spit the beaks into, but many eat the beak. Elder brother suddenly has ten and not twenty left in his jar. One sister comes outside and goes to grab an extra jar before she is caught while trying to get back inside the house. As their arguing begins to hit another level of volume, one of the boys comes out carrying a huge platter of cut watermelon and helim to resounding applause. Bütün deliler toplandı bir yere. *All the mad people have fallen upon one place*

My tongue is lifting my upper lip, pressing against it in sheer focus and maybe out of thirst, too, from wanting the watermelon. A stray dog running past the fence that I'm leaning on barks at me and grabs their attention – I don't want them to see me, so I walk backwards until the bushes hide me better before turning to get home quick.

YUSUF: MOUNTAIN DRIVE, THE NEXT DAY

Yusuf's son-in-law passes him a hollowed-out cabbage with segments of yusufcuk *mandarin* fixed to its sides. Within it are leaves of olive tree pulled from the trees that cover the mountains they'd driven through to get to this patch of mountain. More importantly, the cabbage cup has been filled with enough raisin-smelling zivania to go right to someone's head. They call it doğal bardak, *cup of nature* and as Yusuf goes to take a second sip his phone buzzes so loud in his pocket that his hands shake some of the drink out, and they mourn the droplets he should have caught in his mouth.

The August heat is still aggressive although they left before sunrise to drive to Katara. Before their drive back, the men set up hammocks in the shade and rest while they sing softly. Some of the men sit on deckchairs playing backgammon together, doing their best not to lose their dice in the stream flowing to their left. The water is cold and is used constantly to wet their brainstems. They remind each other of old stories: that time that Yusuf's first casino in Kıbrıs had the American superstar walk in, or when his son in-law broke his little toe trying to milk a goat. Yusuf is sad to recollect the death of his first love, a lady almost his mum's age who was married

Turkish Cypriot

242

off to a man who died in the war. He warns his son-in-law of loving too secretly, so secretly that the only way you can mourn is by giving the mosque money and lokum to read for the diseased. On the plus side, he notes, you can always help the dead by helping the living they leave behind.

DAMLA, SAME DAY, 2012

I watch them on my phone from Anne's small kitchen, a trailer of their day uploaded to Facebook. Steam escapes from Yusuf abi's mouth and I think it is the cold air I'm seeing. From an early age I've been jealous of these men for what they have, like the watermelon. I did ask if I could go along. Yusuf abi's idea of helping me to join in on the fun is by recommending a husband who will join him when he goes out to Kantara.

I'm preparing dinner for İpek and Anne, but can't imagine eating it myself. I put my knife to the fish's head and slice under the gill. Its eyes are clear, saturnine, it is dead because it was born in the wrong month. On her phone, İpek is recording me as I cut the fish's head off while the camera pans around the room. When she settles her focus back on me, my hands are pressed against the scales, trying to keep the fish down as it tries to throw itself off the counter. Anne laughs and comes over, pouring some salt on it.

Very fresh fish still have their neurons intact, even though they're dead. As soon as you add salt to the exposed muscles, the neurons are triggered and the muscles contract. So very dead fish will continue to move about until they use up their store of energy.

—Ne sattan be? *Oi, what you trying to sell?*

Cadaveric spasm, also known as instantaneous rigor, cataleptic rigidity and zombie mode. The exposed muscle is contracting and life is like that, bouncing hopla hopla when you shouldn't.

The dead body forces itself not to forget life; it insists.

Anne has started to fry the fish, and I check my phone. Cemile has followed me on Instagram and her hair is curly in her profile picture. İpek has left me to cut extra onions and I can hear notifications coming through to my phone, I try to cut the onion fine like belly hairs.

from young
we eat with our eyes closed

little sisters sleeping, who's to know?

now we're in water
stirring

hair above the waves, we cool our foreheads,
bank memories in each other

popcorn-ceiling flats;
six controls and don't-touch doors

somewhere my brother, under a shopfront.
somewhere my dad.

stumbling in new places,
snail-eaten cabbage
rolling,

TV on for shelling beans.
TV on for sleeping.

cola-body fruit machine
resting between scheming

swings that rust
hands scuffing
hooks and buzzers
friends by blood

fingers of sunlight
blanket hidden
kids under tents
with ceramic dolls

some pay 10 per cent
some pay it all

flush flush
eavesdropping pipes

washing machine dreaming
here we go again
in marsh cycles

retell it so it's yours, and it's yours now

ACKNOWLEDGEMENTS

As I wrote *Keeping the House*, one of the things that spurred me on was knowing that I had such community around me. With thanks to all those who have supported me on this journey.

Special thanks to my agent Donald Winchester for your patience, time and faith in my work – what a joy it is to be read by you. To the team at And Other Stories for what has been a truly touching publishing experience, I feel very fortunate!

To my editor Max Porter – our conversations have taught me so much. Thank you for encouraging me to make up vocabulary as I go and let this novel be itself.

Endless thanks to Spread the Word. Ruth Harrison. Bobby Nayyar. Tom MacAndrew. Aliya Gulamani. Eva Lewin. Laura Kenwright. From writing me a letter to share with anyone who didn't believe I was actually writing a book, to introducing me to my editor! To the London Writers Awards Literary Fiction squad. Riley Rockford, Sara Jafari, Kira McPherson, Jarred McGinnis, Sofia Fara and Koyer Ahmed. I can't wait to have a shelf with all of our books on it.

To Jacob Sam-La Rose for seeing a poet in me. Your guidance and Barbican Young Poets have truly changed my life. To Rachel Long for your kindness, surrealism nods and reminding me not to judge myself as I write.

Roger Robinson, who helped me to overcome my fear of writing big. Matthew Sperling, for when you said I should consider writing a novel. Deborah Smith, Saba Ahmed and Theodora Danek for teaching me how feminism is sometimes as simple as being kind to yourself. Sophiya Ali for making me think of the 'chairliness' of chairs. Emily Ajgan for your feedback on draft 1. Mr Collins. You inspired me to aim so far, worlds far. Thank you. Many thanks to Arvon for creating a space for me to write amongst trees and daffodils.

Gboyega Odubanjo. Geezer. For our talks about the people in our stories.
Bayan Goudarzpour. Kind as hugs. For such a sensitive sensitivity read.
Richard L. Dixon. Lostintottenham. Photography 'soundtrack' to this book.
Mandisa Apena. Sensitivity reader, inspiration weaver.
Annie Hayter – fog cutter – for being my poetry eye.

Thank you to all those who shared their stories with me and let me into rooms that my imagination couldn't quite paint. We built this book together.

And deep gratitude to my brilliant mother, and my wise sisters and brothers. My first readers and cup-of-tea makers. What a team we are.

Dear readers,

As well as relying on bookshop sales, And Other Stories relies on subscriptions from people like you for many of our books, whose stories other publishers often consider too risky to take on.

Our subscribers don't just make the books physically happen. They also help us approach booksellers, because we can demonstrate that our books already have readers and fans. And they give us the security to publish in line with our values, which are collaborative, imaginative and 'shamelessly literary'.

All of our subscribers:

- receive a first-edition copy of each of the books they subscribe to
- are thanked by name at the end of our subscriber-supported books
- receive little extras from us by way of thank you, for example: postcards created by our authors

BECOME A SUBSCRIBER,
OR GIVE A SUBSCRIPTION TO A FRIEND

Visit andotherstories.org/subscriptions to help make our books happen. You can subscribe to books we're in the process of making. To purchase books we have already published, we urge you to support your local or favourite bookshop and order directly from them – the often unsung heroes of publishing.

OTHER WAYS TO GET INVOLVED

If you'd like to know about upcoming events and reading groups (our foreign-language reading groups help us choose books to publish, for example) you can:

- join our mailing list at: andotherstories.org
- follow us on Twitter: @andothertweets
- join us on Facebook: facebook.com/AndOtherStoriesBooks
- admire our books on Instagram: @andotherpics
- follow our blog: andotherstories.org/ampersand

A Cudmore
Aaron McEnery
Aaron Schneider
Abigail Charlesworth
Abigail Howell
Abigail Walton
Adam Clarke
Adam Duncan
Adam Lenson
Adrian Astur
  Alvarez
Adrian Perez
Aifric Campbell
Aisha McLean
Ajay Sharma
Alan Baldwin
Alan McMonagle
Alan Stoskopf
Alastair Gillespie
Alastair Whitson
Albert Puente
Alecia Marshall
Aleksi Rennes
Alex Fleming
Alex Hoffman
Alex Liebman
Alex Lockwood
Alex Pearce
Alex Ramsey
Alexander Barbour
Alexander Bunin
Alexander Leggatt
Alexander Williams
Alexandra Citron
Alexandra Stewart
Alexandra Stewart
Alexandra Tilden
Alexandra Webb
Alfred Birnbaum
Alfred Tobler
Ali Ersahin
Ali Riley
Ali Smith
Ali Usman
Alice Morgan
Alice Radosh
Alice Shumate
Alice Smith
Alicia Medina
Alison Hardy
Alison Lock
Alison Winston
Aliya Rashid
Alyse Ceirante
Alyssa Rinaldi
Alyssa Tauber
Amado Floresca
Amaia Gabantxo
Amalia Gladhart
Amanda

Amanda María
  Izquierdo
  Gonzalez
Amanda Read
Amelia Lowe
Amine Hamadache
Amy and Jamie
Amy Arnold
Amy Benson
Amy Bessent
Amy Bojang
Amy Finch
Amy Tabb
Ana Novak
Anastasia Carver
Andrea Barlien
Andrea Brownstone
Andrea Oyarzabal
  Koppes
Andrea Reece
Andrew Kerr-Jarrett
Andrew Marston
Andrew McCallum
Andrew Ratomski
Andrew Rego
Andy Corsham
Andy Marshall
Andy Turner
Aneesa Higgins
Angela Everitt
Angela Lopez
Angelica Ribichini
Angus Walker
Anita Starosta
Anna Finneran
Anna Hawthorne
Anna Milsom
Anna Zaranko
Anne Barnes
Anne Boileau Clarke
Anne Carus
Anne Craven
Anne Edyvean
Anne Frost
Anne Magnier-
  Redon
Anne O' Brien
Anne Ryden
Anne Sticksel
Annie McDermott
Anonymous
Anonymous
Anthony Alexander
Anthony Brown
Anthony Cotton
Anthony Quinn
Antonia Lloyd-Jones
Antonia Saske
Antony Osgood
Antony Pearce

Aoife Boyd
Archie Davies
Arthur John Rowles
Asako Serizawa
Ash Lazarus
Audrey Mash
Audrey Small
Aysha Powell
Barbara Bettsworth
Barbara Mellor
Barbara Robinson
Barbara Spicer
Barbara Wheatley
Barry Norton
Barry Watkinson
Barry John Fletcher
Bea Karol Burks
Becky Cherriman
Ben Buchwald
Ben Schofield
Ben Thornton
Ben Walter
Benjamin Judge
Benjamin Pester
Bethan Kent
Bhakti Gajjar
Bianca Duec
Bianca Jackson
Bianca Winter
Bill Fletcher
Bjørnar Djupevik
  Hagen
Blazej Jedras
Briallen Hopper
Brian Anderson
Brian Byrne
Brian Callaghan
Brian Conn
Brian Smith
Bridget Maddison
Brigita Ptackova
Burkhard Fehsenfeld
Caitlin Halpern
Callie Steven
Cameron Adams
Camilla Imperiali
Carla Castanos
Carly Willis
Carol Quintana
Carole Parkhouse
Carolina Pineiro
Caroline Lodge
Caroline Perry
Caroline Smith
Caroline West
Catharine Braithwaite
Catherine Cleary
Catherine Tandy
Catherine Lambert
Catherine Tolo

Catherine
  Williamson
Cathryn Siegal-
  Bergman
Cathy Galvin
Cathy Sowell
Catie Kosinski
Catriona Gibbs
Cecilia Rossi
Cecilia Uribe
Chantal Lyons
Chantal Wright
Charlene Huggins
Charles Fernyhough
Charles Kovach
Charles Dee Mitchell
Charles Rowe
Charles Watson
Charlie Errock
Charlie Levin
Charlie Small
Charlotte Bruton
Charlotte Coulthard
Charlotte Holtam
Charlotte Ryland
Charlotte Smith
Charlotte Whittle
Chelsey Johnson
Cherise Wolas
China Miéville
Chris Gostick
Chris Gribble
Chris Holmes
Chris Johnstone
Chris Köpruner
Chris Potts
Chris Stergalas
Chris Stevenson
Chris Thornton
Christian
  Schuhmann
Christine Elliott
Christine Humphreys
Christine Stickler
Christopher Allen
Christopher Homfray
Christopher Jenkin
Christopher Smith
Christopher Stout
Ciara Ní Riáin
Ciarán Schütte
Claire Adams
Claire Brooksby
Claire Hayward
Claire Morrison
Claire Morrison
Claire Smith
Claire Williams
Clarice Borges
Clarissa Pattern

Cliona Quigley
Colin Denyer
Colin Hewlett
Colin Matthews
Collin Brooke
Cornelia Svedman
Courtney Lilly
CP Hunter
Craig Kennedy
Cynthia De La Torre
Cyrus Massoudi
Daisy Savage
Dale Wisely
Dan Martin
Dan Parkinson
Daniel Arnold
Daniel Coxon
Daniel Gillespie
Daniel Hahn
Daniel Hester-Smith
Daniel Stewart
Daniel Syrovy
Daniel Venn
Daniela Steierberg
Darina Brejtrova
Darryll Rogers
Dave Ashley
Dave Hill
Dave Lander
David Anderson
David Ball
David Coates
David Cowan
David Darvasi
David Davies
David Gould
David Greenlaw
David Gunnarsson
David Hebblethwaite
David Higgins
David Hodges
David Johnson-
  Davies
David Kinnaird
David Leverington
David F Long
David McIntyre
David Miller
David and Lydia Pell
David Reid
David Richardson
David Shriver
David Smith
Dawn Bass
Dean Stokes
Dean Taucher
Deb Unferth
Debbie Pinfold
Deborah Banks
Declan Gardner

Declan O'Driscoll
Deirdre Nic
  Mhathuna
Delaina Haslam
Denis Larose
Denise Bretländer
Denise Carstensen
Denton Djurasevich
Derek Taylor-
  Vrsalovich
Desiree Mason
Diana Baker Smith
Diana Digges
Dietrich Menzel
Dina Abdul-Wahab
Dinesh Prasad
Dirk Hanson
Dominic Nolan
Dominick Santa
  Cattarina
Dominique Brocard
Dorothy Bottrell
Doug Wallace
Duncan Clubb
Duncan Macgregor
Duncan Marks
Dustin Hackfeld
Dustin Haviv
Dyanne Prinsen
Earl James
Ebba Aquila
Ebba Tornérhielm
Ed Tronick
Ekaterina Beliakova
Elaine Frances
Elaine Juzl
Eleanor Maier
Elena Esparza
Elif Aganoglu
Elina Zicmane
Elisabeth Cook
Elizabeth Braswell
Elizabeth Coombes
Elizabeth Draper
Elizabeth Franz
Elizabeth Guss
Elizabeth Leach
Elizabeth Seals
Ellen Beardsworth
Ellen Casey
Ellen Wilkinson
Ellie Goddard
Ellie Small
Emeline Morin
Emily Armitage
Emily Dixon
Emily Jang
Emily Webber
Emily Williams
Emma Bielecki

Emma Dell
Emma Louise Grove
Emma Musty
Emma Page
Emma Post
Emma Reynolds
Emma Teale
Emma Turesson
Eric Tucker
Erica Mason
Erin Cameron Allen
Erin Louttit
Esmée de Heer
Esther Donnelly
Esther Kinsky
Etta Searle
Eugene O'Hare
Eunji Kim
Eva Mitchell
Eva Oddo
Ewan Tant
F Gary Knapp
Fawzia Kane
Fay Barrett
Faye Williams
Felicity Williams
Felix Valdivieso
Finbarr Farragher
Fiona Liddle
Fiona Mozley
Fiona Quinn
Fran Sanderson
Frances
  Christodoulou
Frances Spangler
Frances Thiessen
Francesca Hemery
Francis Mathias
François von Hurter
Frank van Orsouw
Freddie Radford
Freya Killilea-Clark
Friederike Knabe
Gabriel Colnic
Gabriel and Mary de
  Courcy Cooney
Gala Copley
Garan Holcombe
Gary Kavanagh
Gavin Aitchison
Gavin Collins
Gavin Smith
Gawain Espley
Gemma Bird
Gemma Doyle
Genaro Palomo Jr
Genevieve Lewington
Geoff Fisher
Geoff Thrower
Geoffrey Cohen

Geoffrey Urland
George McCaig
George Stanbury
George Wilkinson
Georgia Panteli
Georgia Shomidie
Georgia Wall
Georgina Hildick-
  Smith
Georgina Norton
Geraldine Brodie
Gerry Craddock
Gill Boag-Munroe
Gillian Grant
Gina Heathcote
Glen Bornais
Glenn Russell
Gordon Cameron
Gosia Pennar
Grace Cohen
Graham Blenkinsop
Graham R Foster
Graham Page
Gregory Philp
Hadil Balzan
Halina Schiffman-
  Shilo
Hamish Russell
Hannah Bucknell
Hannah Freeman
Hannah Harford-
  Wright
Hannah Jane
  Lownsbrough
Hannah Morris
Hannah Procter
Hannah Rapley
Hanora Bagnell
Hans Lazda
Harriet Stiles
Haydon Spenceley
Hayley Cox
Hazel Smoczynska
Hector Judd
Heidi James
Helen Bailey
Helen Berry
Helen Brady
Helen Coombes
Helen Moor
Helena Buffery
Henrietta Dunsmuir
Henriette
  Magerstaedt
Henrike Laehnemann
Henry Patino
Hilary Munro
HJ Fotheringham
Holly Barker
Holly Down

Howard Robinson
Hyoung-Won Park
I K E Lehvonen
Ian Hagues
Ian McMillan
Ian Mond
Ian Randall
Ian Whiteley
Ida Grochowska
Ifer Moore
Ilona Abb
Ines Alfano
Iona Preston
Iona Stevens
Irene Mansfield
Irina Tzanova
Isabella Garment
Isabella Weibrecht
Isobel Dixon
Isobel Foxford
J Drew Hancock-
 Teed
Jacinta Perez Gavilan
 Torres
Jack Brown
Jacob Blizard
Jacqueline Haskell
Jacqueline Lademann
Jacqui Jackson
Jade Yiu
Jadie Lee
Jaelen Hartwin
Jake Baldwinson
James Attlee
James Avery
James Beck
James Crossley
James Cubbon
James Dahm
James Lehmann
James Leonard
James Lesniak
James Norman
James Portlock
James Scudamore
James Silvestro
Jamie Cox
Jamie Walsh
Jan Hicks
Jane Anderton
Jane Dolman
Jane Fairweather
Jane Roberts
Jane Roberts
Jane Willborn
Jane Woollard
Janelle Ward
Janne Støen
Jasmine Gideon
Jason Calloway

Jason Grunebaum
Jason Lever
Jason Montano
Jason Timermanis
Jayne Watson
JE Crispin
Jeanne Guyon
Jeff Collins
Jeff Goguen
Jeffrey Coleman
Jen Calleja
Jen Hardwicke
Jenifer Logie
Jennifer Arnold
Jennifer Fisher
Jennifer Mills
Jennifer Watts
Jenny Barlow
Jenny Huth
Jenny Newton
Jeremy Koenig
Jeremy Wellens
Jess Hazlewood
Jess Wood
Jesse Coleman
Jesse Hara
Jesse Thayre
Jessica Cooper
Jessica Gately
Jessica Kibler
Jessica Martin
Jessica Queree
Jessica Mello
Jethro Soutar
Jo Cox
Jo Elliot
Jo Keyes
Joanna Luloff
Joanne Smith
Joao Pedro Bragatti
 Winckler
JoDee Brandon
Jodie Adams
Joe Huggins
Joel Garza
Joel Swerdlow
Joelle Young
Johanna Eliasson
Johannes Menzel
Johannes Georg Zipp
John Bennett
John Berube
John Bogg
John Conway
John Down
John Gent
John Guyatt
John Hanson
John Hodgson
John Kelly

John Reid
John Royley
John Shaw
John Steigerwald
John Walsh
John Winkelman
John Wyatt
Jolene Smith
Jon Riches
Jonathan Blaney
Jonathan Fiedler
Jonathan Harris
Jonathan Huston
Jonny Kiehlmann
Jordana Carlin
Jorid Martinsen
Jose Machado
Joseph Novak
Joseph Schreiber
Joseph Thomas
Josh Calvo
Josh Sumner
Joshua Davis
Joshua McNamara
Joy Paul
Judith Gruet-Kaye
Judy Davies
Julia Rochester
Julia Sanches
Julia Sutton-
 Mattocks
Julia Von Dem
 Knesebeck
Julian Hemming
Julian Hemming
Julian Molina
Julie Greenwalt
Julie Winter
Juliet Birkbeck
Juliet Swann
Jupiter Jones
Juraj Janik
Justine Sherwood
Kaarina Hollo
Kaelyn Davis
Kaja R Anker-Rasch
Kasper Haakansson
Kataline Lukacs
Katarzyna
 Bartoszynska
Kate Attwooll
Kate Beswick
Kate Carlton-Reditt
Kate Gardner
Kate Procter
Kate Shires
Katharina Liehr
Katharine Robbins
Katherine
 Mackinnon

Katherine Sotejeff-
 Wilson
Kathryn Edwards
Kathryn Oliver
Kathryn Williams
Kathy Gogarty
Katia Wengraf
Katie Brown
Katie Freeman
Katie Grant
Katie Kennedy
Katie Kline
Katie Smart
Katy Robinson
Keith Walker
Kelly Mehring
Kelly Souza
Ken Barlow
Kenneth Blythe
Kenneth Michaels
Kent McKernan
Kerry Parke
Kieran Rollin
Kieron James
Kim McGowan
Kim Metcalf
Kim White
Kirsten Hey
Kirsty Doole
Kirsty Simpkins
KJ Buckland
KL Ee
Kris Ann Trimis
Kristen Tcherneshoff
Kristin Djuve
Krystale Tremblay-
 Moll
Krystine Phelps
Kyra Wilder
Kysanna Shawney
Lacy Wolfe
Lana Selby
Lara Vergnaud
Larry Wikoff
Laura Batatota
Laura Pugh
Laura Rangeley
Laura Zlatos
Lauren Rea
Laurence Laluyaux
Leah Zamesnik
Leanne Radojkovich
Lee Harbour
Leon Geis
Leona Iosifidou
Leslie Jacobson
Liliana Lobato
Lily Blacksell
Linda Jones
Lindsay Brammer

Lindsey Ford
Lindsey Stuart
Linette Arthurton
  Bruno
Lisa Agostini
Lisa Barnard
Lisa Bean
Lisa Dillman
Lisa Leahigh
Lisa Simpson
Liz Clifford
Liz Ketch
Liz Starbuck Greer
Liz Wilding
Lorna Bleach
Lottie Smith
Louise Evans
Louise Greenberg
Louise Hoelscher
Louise Jolliffe
Louise Smith
Luc Daley
Luc Verstraete
Lucie Taylor
Lucy Gorman
Lucy Greaves
Lucy Leeson-Smith
Lucy Moffatt
Lucy Banks
Ludmilla Jordanova
Luke Healey
Luke Loftiss
Luna Esmerode
Lydia Trethewey
Lynn Fung
Lynn Martin
Lynn Ross
Maeve Lambe
Magdaline Rohweder
Maggie Kerkman
Maggie Livesey
Mags Lewis
Mahan L Ellison &
  K Ashley Dickson
Malgorzata Rokicka
Mandy Wight
Marcel Inhoff
Marcel Schlamowitz
Marco Medjimorec
Margaret Cushen
Margaret Jull Costa
Margo Gorman
Mari Troskie
Maria Ahnhem
  Farrar
Maria Hill
Maria Lomunno
Maria Losada
Maria Quevedo
Maria Pia Tissot

Marie Cloutier
Marie Donnelly
Marina Castledine
Mario Sifuentez
Marisa Wilson
Marja S Laaksonen
Mark Harris
Mark Huband
Mark Sargent
Mark Scott
Mark Sheets
Mark Sztyber
Mark Waters
Mark Walsh
Marlene Adkins
Martin Brown
Martin Munro
Martin Price
Martin Eric Rodgers
Mary Angela
  Brevidoro
Mary Heiss
Mary Wang
Maryse Meijer
Mathias Ruthner
Mathieu Trudeau
Matt Davies
Matt Greene
Matt O'Connor
Matthew Adamson
Matthew Armstrong
Matthew Banash
Matthew Eatough
Matthew Francis
Matthew Gill
Matthew Lowe
Matthew Warshauer
Matthew Woodman
Matthias Rosenberg
Maura Cheeks
Maureen Pritchard
Max Cairnduff
Max Longman
Maya Chung
Meaghan Delahunt
Meg Lovelock
Megan Holt
Megan Wittling
Mel Pryor
Melissa Beck
Melissa da Silveira
  Serpa
Melissa Quignon-
  Finch
Melissa Stogsdill
Melissa Wan
Melynda Nuss
Meredith Jones
Mia Khachidze
Michael Aguilar

Michael Bichko
Michael Boog
Michael James
  Eastwood
Michael Gavin
Michael Kuhn
Michael Moran
Michael Pollak
Michael Roess
Michael
  Schneiderman
Michelle Perkins
Miguel Head
Miles Smith-Morris
Moira Sweeney
Moira Weir
Mollie Chandler
Molly Foster
Mona Arshi
Moray Teale
Morayma Jimenez
Moremi Apata-
  Omisore
Morgan Lyons
Moriah Haefner
MP Boardman
Muireann Maguire
Myles Nolan
N Tsolak
Nan Craig
Nancy Jacobson
Nancy Oakes
Nancy Sosnow
Nanda Griffioen
Natalia Reyes
Natalie Ricks
Nathalie Atkinson
Nathalie Karagiannis
Nathan McNamara
Nathan Rowley
Nathan Weida
Neferti Tadiar
Nguyen Phan
Nicholas Brown
Nicholas Rutherford
Nicholas Smith
Nick Chapman
Nick James
Nick Love
Nick Nelson &
  Rachel Eley
Nick Sidwell
Nick Twemlow
Nicola Cook
Nicola Hart
Nicola Mira
Nicola Sandiford
Nicola Scott
Nicole Joy
Nicole Matteini

Nigel Fishburn
Niki Sammut
Nina Alexandersen
Nina de la Mer
Nina Todorova
Nina Nickerson
Odilia Corneth
Olga Zilberbourg
Olivia Scott
Olivia Turon
Pamela Ritchie
Pamela Tao
Pat Bevins
Patricia Aronsson
Patrick Hawley
Paul Brackenridge
Paul Cray
Paul Jones
Paul Munday
Paul Myatt
Paul Robinson
Paul Scott
Paul Segal
Paul Wright
Paul Thompson and
  Gordon McArthur
Pauline Drury
Pauline France
Pavlos Stavropoulos
Penelope Hewett
  Brown
Peter Griffin
Peter Halliday
Peter Hudson
Peter McBain
Peter McCambridge
Peter Rowland
Peter Taplin
Peter Van de Maele
  and Narina Dahms
Peter Watson
Peter Wells
Petra Stapp
Phil Bartlett
Philip Herbert
Philip Nulty
Philip Warren
Philip Williams
Philipp Jarke
Phillipa Clements
Phoebe Millerwhite
Phyllis Reeve
Pia Figge
Piet Van Bockstal
PRAH Foundation
Prakash Nayak
Rachael de Moravia
Rachael Williams
Rachel Andrews
Rachel Carter

Rachel Darnley-Smith
Rachel Dolan
Rachel Matheson
Rachel Van Riel
Rachel Watkins
Ralph Cowling
Ramona Pulsford
Ranbir Sidhu
Raymond Manzo
Rebecca Braun
Rebecca Carter
Rebecca Fearnley
Rebecca Ketcherside
Rebecca Micklewright
Rebecca Moss
Rebecca O'Reilly
Rebecca Peer
Rebecca Rose
Rebecca Rosenthal
Rebecca Shaak
Rebekka Bremmer
Renee Thomas
Rhiannon Armstrong
Rich Sutherland
Richard Catty
Richard Clark
Richard Ellis
Richard Gwyn
Richard Mansell
Richard Padwick
Richard Priest
Richard Sanders
Richard Santos
Richard Shea
Richard Soundy
Richard White
Riley & Alyssa Manning
Rishi Dastidar
Rita Kaar
Rita O'Brien
Robert Gillett
Robert Hamilton
Robert Hannah
Robert Sliman
Robin McLean
Robin Taylor
Rogelio Pardo
Roger Newton
Roger Ramsden
Rory Williamson
Ros Woolner
Rosalind May
Rosalind Ramsay
Rose Crichton

Rose Pearce
Rosie Pinhorn
Ross MacIntyre
Roxanne O'Del Ablett
Roz Simpson
Ruby Thiagarajan
Rupert Ziziros
Ruth Deyermond
Ruth Field
Ryan Day
Sabine Little
Sakshi Surana
Sally Arkinstall
Sally Baker
Sally Bramley
Sally Ellis
Sally Foreman
Sally Warner
Sam Gordon
Sam Reese
Samantha Walton
Samuel Crosby
Sara Bea
Sara Cheraghlou
Sara Kittleson
Sara Sherwood
Sara Warshawski
Sarah Arboleda
Sarah Blunden
Sarah Brewer
Sarah Goddard
Sarah Lucas
Sarah Morton
Sarah Pybus
Sarah Roff
Sarah Spitz
Scott Astrada
Scott Chiddister
Scott Henkle
Scott Russell
Scott Simpson
Sean Birnie
Sean Kottke
Sean McDonagh
Sean McGivern
Serena Chang
Shane Horgan
Shannon Knapp
Sharon Dogar
Sharon McCammon
Shauna Gilligan
Sheila Packa
Sheryl Jermyn
Shira Lob
Sian Hannah
Sienna Kang

Simon James
Simon Pitney
Simon Robertson
Siriol Hugh-Jones
SK Grout
Sonia McLintock
Sophia Wickham
Sophie Church
ST Dabbagh
Stacy Rodgers
Stefanie Schrank
Stefano Mula
Stephan Eggum
Stephanie Lacava
Stephanie Shields
Stephanie Smee
Stephen Pearsall
Steve Chapman
Steve Dearden
Steve James
Steve Raby
Steven Norton
Stewart Eastham
Stu Hennigan
Stu Sherman
Stuart Grey
Stuart Phillips
Stuart Snelson
Stuart Wilkinson
Su Bonfanti
Sunny Payson
Susan Clegg
Susan Edsall
Susan Jaken
Susan Winter
Suzanne Colangelo Lillis
Sydney Hutchinson
Sylvie Zannier-Betts
Tamara Larsen
Tania Hershman
Tara Pahari
Tara Roman
Tasmin Maitland
Teresa Werner
Teri Hoskin
Tess Cohen
Tess McAlister
Tessa Lang
Thom Cuell
Thom Keep
Thomas Mitchell
Thomas Phipps
Thomas Rasmussen
Thomas Smith
Thomas van den Bout

Thomas Andrew White
Tiffany Lehr
Tim & Cynthia
Tim Kelly
Tim Schneider
Tim Scott
Tim Theroux
Tina Andrews
Tina Rotherham-Winqvist
Toby Halsey
Toby Ryan
Tom Darby
Tom Doyle
Tom Franklin
Tom Gray
Tom and Ben Knight
Tom Stafford
Tom Whatmore
Tory Jeffay
Tracy Heuring
Tracy Northup
Tracy Shapley
Trevor Wald
Ursula Dawson
Val & Tom Flechtner
Valerie O'Riordan
Vanessa Fuller
Vanessa Heggie
Vanessa Nolan
Veronica Barnsley
Victor Meadowcroft
Victoria Eld
Victoria Goodbody
Victoria Huggins
Victoria Larroque
Vijay Pattisapu
Vikki O'Neill
Wendy Langridge
Will Herbert
Will Stolton
William Black
William Dennehy
William Franklin
William Mackenzie
William Sitters
Xanthe Rendall
Yana Ellis
Yoora Yi Tenen
Zachary Hope
Zachary Maricondia
Zareena Amiruddin
Zoë Brasier